Fly Home, Butterfly

Fly Home, Butterfly

In Search of a Father

— A Novel —

LINDA L. GRAHAM

LUMINARE PRESS
WWW.LUMINAREPRESS.COM

Fly Home, Butterfly: In Search of a Father
Copyright © 2021 by Linda L. Graham

All rights reserved. This book or any portion thereof may not be reproduced or used in any manner whatsoever without the express written permission of the publisher, except for the use of brief quotations in a book review.

Printed in the United States of America

Luminare Press
442 Charnelton St.
Eugene, OR 97401
www.luminarepress.com

LCCN: 2021918067
ISBN: 978-1-64388-789-0

With love to Raul

You are always there for me.

Contents

Characters x

U.S. and Mexico Map xi

Prologue 1

Part 1—Texas 29

Part 2—Mexico 99

Part 3—Oregon 201

Epilogue 229

Acknowledgements 231

Bibliography 232

Author's Note 233

This book is a work of fiction. Names, characters, businesses, organizations, places, events, and incidents either are the product of the author's imagination or are used fictitiously. Any resemblance to actual persons, living or dead, events, or locales is entirely coincidental.

Also by Linda L. Graham

INDIANA SUMMER:
From Cornfields and Lightning Bugs
A Memoir

TWO MICE AND A DRAGONFLY:
How Cats Help a Disconnected Family
A Novel

Characters

Casandra (Cassie) McMillen—adopted daughter of Tully
Tully McMillen—Cassie's adoptive mother
Jasmine McMillen—Cassie's adoptive sister
Sebastian and Mandy—Tully's cats
Stephanie Hoffman—Cassie's birth mother
Robert Harris—Cassie's estranged birth father
Preston Chang and Claire Middleton—friends of Cassie
Tina—waitress
Dr. Jordan—retired professor from Oregon State
Dominican—Dr. Jordan's cat
Ramon and Angel—men from South Padre Island
Sarah Guthrow—Cassie's biological aunt
Kevin Guthrow—Cassie's cousin
Guy Collins—friend of Dr. Jordan
Janice—Cassie's editor
Luis Mendez—Cassie's boyfriend
Esteban, Marie, Mercedes, and Vivian Mendez—Luis' family
Joan—cat sitter
Juan and Jose—trail guides
Jason and Andrew—casual friends from Cassie's work
John—Jasmine's husband
Josh and Josie—Jasmine's children
Uncle Luke
Joe and Alicia—nurse and journalist

U.S. and Mexico Map

(North America-PICRYL Public Domain Image)

PROLOGUE

Cassie's Wanderings

2017

> "Like a butterfly stuck in a chrysalis, waiting for the perfect moment, I was waiting for the day I could burst forth and fly away and find my home."
>
> —EMME ROLLINS, OUR ROCK STAR

It's been twelve years. Here I am again, home at last in the kitchen of Tully, my adoptive mom. Her house is a different one, in a new location, and is much smaller than before. It's a condo actually. However, her kitchen, although not as spacious as before, is arranged the same way. The gray earthenware canister holds wooden spoons, spatulas, and a wire whisk. I never once saw her whisk anything, but it takes its rightful place in the jar. Mom's stainless toaster sits on the cabinet near her refrigerator, same as always. The dishes in the cabinet are the identical white Corelle Ware as from years before. Mom grins widely at me as she takes out a fork to whip up scrambled eggs, adding a little milk first. The milk is her secret to fluffy eggs, and she has always cooked them that way except for deviled eggs at Easter.

Sebastian and Mandy sidle in, begging for food as they predictably do whenever Mom cooks. Funny though—she feeds them only dry or wet cat food, never human food. They smell her cooking and ask anyway. I doubt that they would touch human food if she put some down for them. I tried to once with Penelope, but she sniffed and turned away. Penelope was my childhood nanny cat. Mom has always had cats in her home ever since I was one year old, and she told me she has always had cats, even before I came along. Penelope was Jasmine's nanny cat too. Jasmine is four years younger than I, my adoptive sister, and parents' biological child. I was one year old when Tully and Sean brought me to live with them and later adopted me. Now Jasmine is married to John and they have two young children, Josh and Josie. I will be thirty-three next month—no longer a young thing, but not old yet either.

"Here's your breakfast, Cassie. Served with love." I was finally home again after wandering for years, searching for my real dad. Even though I left home at eighteen to discover my real mom, when I found her, it only created more questions as to who I am and why. I know now that it all doesn't really matter when you have a home to come back to, but I had to find out for myself. Along the way, I too, found lasting love, but I digress.

Where do I begin? I suppose my journey begins shortly after my adopted dad, Sean, died of a heart attack. At the time, I still lived in Montana, but came back to Springville, Washington for the funeral. After that, I arranged with my employer to transfer me back home to Springville. A year later, I decided to search for my biological dad. I didn't even know his name at the time, so of course, I had to return to Bozeman and ask my birth mother, Stephanie.

Chapter 1
2005

I awoke with a start in the semi-darkness, at first disoriented as to where I was. Then the odor of stale cigarette smoke and sour alcohol reminded me. Right. I was back in Stephanie's single-wide manufactured home. The home afforded two cramped bedrooms with a tiny bathroom in between. I slept in the extra bedroom, which was chuck full of boxes surrounding a twin bed. I groped for the light switch. The clock on the nightstand read 6:00 a.m., but it was still dark out. I had arrived yesterday and had tried to revive Stephanie enough to ask her questions about my real father. I replayed the conversation in my mind, still pondering the possibilities, and thinking of more questions than answers.

Once more I had returned to Bozeman, Montana to visit Stephanie, my biological mom. I had been so disappointed when I had first found her two years ago. At that time, I could hardly wait to see her and get acquainted. I had thought that at last, I would discover my true identity and roots.

What a joke. I had eventually found her in this run-down, filthy home in a trailer park. Again, I knocked on her door. "Stephanie, are you there?" I called out. No answer. I jiggled the door handle and the door swung open. There she lay, passed out on her ugly brown, threadbare sofa. The empty vodka bottle lying on the floor told her story. "Stephanie, it's me, your daughter, Cassie." I replayed the meeting of Stephanie over and over in my mind. Here I was again in her shanty of a home, still trying to figure things out.

"Huh? Who are you and why the hell are you in my house?" Stephanie's voice cracked as she looked up at me once more with glazed-over eyes, dark circles surrounding them like racoon markings. Her hair was a stringy, long, peroxide-blonde mess, longer and coarser than before. She was in the exact same place, passed out on the same ugly sofa, as when I first found her living here. Nothing had changed, with the exception that she appeared even more emaciated or shrunken. The old feeling of revulsion rose up my throat; I could taste the bile with it. She sickened me.

"I'll make you some coffee, and then we can talk," I said, throwing my overnight bag onto the empty chair next to the sofa.

"Go away. I have nothing more to say to you." Stephanie turned her face toward the back of the couch, pulling the blanket up over her bony shoulders. I chose to ignore that and searched around in her kitchen cabinet until I found the coffee. Soon, the sharp aroma of freshly brewed coffee cleared the stale cigarette stench somewhat. I hoped it would help to rouse her up a bit.

That was yesterday. I decided to stay over another night to try again. Maybe today I could get her to recall something, anything, about who my biological father was or is. One thing I knew from my own dark skin—he was African American, since Stephanie definitely was not. That should narrow things down for her somewhat, even though she had entertained a steady stream of men who slept here over the years.

The early morning was chilly, so I got up and threw on a tattered house robe I found in the closet. It was early November, and the days were short and cold here in Montana. I stumbled into the kitchen area, and saw Stephanie still on the sofa, passed out from her nightly binge. I started coffee and looked around for something to eat. Inside the refrigerator were some eggs and a half loaf of bread, so I began scrambling eggs and popped two slices of bread in the toaster. At least, if Stephanie could eat, she might become a little more coherent. The TV was still on, so I turned it to the morning news, and turned up the volume, hoping that would help rouse her. I kept looking at her for signs of awakening—finally, I saw her eyelids flutter. "Good morning, Stephanie. I made us breakfast."

"Wha-what? I don't eat breakfast. Forget it," she said, slurring her words a little, her tongue obviously dry from sleeping with her mouth open.

"Today is different. We are going to eat breakfast together, and I made some fresh coffee." I tried to sound chirpy and positive but saw that it wasn't having much effect. Stephanie had already turned to face the back of the sofa again. "Come on. Time to rise and shine. I don't know when you have to go to work, so I wanted to make sure we had enough time to talk."

"Talk? Talk about what?" Her voice was muffled into the sofa, but at least she was speaking.

"First, let's get you up to the table. Maybe you need to splash water on your face before we sit down." I took hold of her by the elbow, bringing her into a sitting position. She didn't seem to resist and sat up obediently. I led her into the bathroom and shut the door behind me. I poured two cups of coffee and set the table, waiting for her to come back out.

After a few minutes, I heard the toilet flush and she emerged, still bleary eyed and disheveled, but at least she was walking on her own without stumbling. She plopped down heavily onto a chair, grabbing one of the coffee mugs, and drew a long sip. "Hot," she commented.

"Right. I just brewed it. Here are some eggs to work on. Then we chat."

"Chat? I have nothing to say. Just leave me alone. I don't see why you keep showing up here. My life is the same, with no room for you in it. Never did have room. Why do you think I gave you up?" Stephanie frowned at me. Her statement would have hurt me two years ago, but I was over it now. I just needed information from her and then I would be out of here. I let the hurtful comment hang in the air as both of us ate in silence. All that could be heard was the scraping of forks on plates. Hurriedly, I finished, and jumped up to clear the dishes. I refilled our mugs, and then sat with my coffee cup in hand.

"Okay. Stephanie, it's time for you to tell me something about my real father. Who is he, how did you meet, and where is he now?"

At that, Stephanie guffawed. "Hell, if I know, kid. You know my lifestyle. We were never married or even an item, you know what I mean? Not even sure who it would be. Why does it matter anyway? Whoever he was, or is, he never cared about you. Why do you care about him?"

"You must have some idea who you were 'seeing' at the time I was conceived. Right?"

"Girl, you are so naïve. It could've been any number of men."

"Stephanie," I persisted, "look at me. Look at me hard. Who did you sleep with who had skin like mine? Huh?" Stephanie snorted, and drank more coffee. "Come on, think!"

"Why should I? I don't owe you anything. You've had a great life living with that family, whatever their names are. Right? Let's not get something going that shouldn't happen. Leave him in peace." Stephanie's face closed. She had had enough. She got up and rummaged around in her cabinet over the sink for another bottle of vodka. She poured out a little of the clear liquid in a glass, lifted it to her lips, and swallowed.

"Don't you have to go into work at the restaurant? Stop drinking. Talk to me."

"I'll call in. This upsets me. Go away and don't come back."

"Stephanie, no! Don't do this. I must know! I have to figure out who I am, don't you see? Please, Stephanie. Tell me." Tears formed in my eyes despite how hard I tried to keep them in check. I was begging, pleading at this point. She was the only one who could possibly help me.

"Alright, alright. But I need my comfort to talk. Don't say I didn't warn you not to dig into the past."

Chapter 2

Stephanie swallowed the shot of vodka in one huge gulp. So far, she didn't finish the scrambled eggs I had cooked for her. She grabbed the bottle, took a swig, and set it down with a loud belch. "Excuse me. So, you want to know about your father, do you? How old are you again? I need to work backwards in my mind."

"Well, I turned twenty-one in July." I made the mistake of staring at her vodka bottle.

"Oh well, congratulations. That entitles you to a celebratory drink with your mother, don't you think?" Stephanie grinned for the first time since I had arrived and pushed the bottle towards me. Awkward. I had never tasted vodka before and wasn't sure I wanted to try it for the first time today. But then again, maybe it would help her to talk.

"Uh, okay, if you're sure. But only a tiny sip. I want to keep my mind clear for our conversation." I tilted the bottle ever so slightly and touched the clear liquid to my lips. I opened my mouth to allow a small amount in and swallowed. It burned all the way down. I coughed and took a swallow of coffee to quell the fire. "Wow! That delivers a punch!" I set the bottle back down in front of Stephanie. Quickly she took another long draw off the bottle.

"Heh, heh. Now that's my girl. Where were we?"

"You're going to think backwards to when I may have been conceived, and I'm twenty-one. So about twenty-two years ago. Black man, no doubt, after seeing how I turned out."

"Well, let me see." Stephanie lifted her chin to stare at the ceiling, as if locating the memory from afar. "He wouldn't have been the only black guy I ever slept with, you know. But twenty-two years… that would be in 1983, right, Cassie?" Surprisingly, she seemed clear headed enough to do the math.

"Right. I was born in '84, remember?"

"Oh yes. At the time, I was living in Springville. I had been living with my parents in Seattle, but they kicked me out when I turned seventeen, saying I was a bad influence on my younger sister. So, I gladly moved out, and relocated in Springville to get away from them completely. My first job was at a coffee shop there. I shared an apartment with a coworker, and you were born when I was barely nineteen. I had no way to support you, so I gave you up."

My heart lurched when she admitted that. I felt so unwanted, so unloved, all over again. How long would it continue to hurt me? I tried to keep a straight face—to show no emotion. I would start today—now, to stop feeling the pain. "So, who did you sleep with then? What was he like? What do you remember about him? How can I get in touch with him? And do I have grandparents in Seattle then?"

"Hey, girl, slow down. One question at a time. It's been a long time ago, you know. I have to work this out in my mind. And no, you don't have grandparents there anymore—at least, not from my side. Both of my parents are dead now." Stephanie sat, sipping slowly now on the vodka, allowing the alcohol to have its effect. "I guess it would've been when I first began working at the café in Springville. Guys came in, lonely, wanting someone to talk to. I was new, and wanted to develop regulars so I could make more in tips, you know? There was this one, tall, dark, and definitely handsome." She chuckled at her own joke about him being tall and dark. "He started coming in everyday and ordering the same breakfast. He always sat in my section. We hit it off after a while and he found out when my shift was up, so we started meeting in the corner booth after work.

"So, what was he like? I mean, what did he do for a living?" I interjected, trying to get to information I could use to find him.

Stephanie glared at me. "I'm getting to all that. My mind works in an orderly way, you know?" She was drinking from a shot glass by this time and poured another. "As I recall, he was a university student. Let's see, what was he studying?" Stephanie raised her eyes to the ceiling, pondering her own question. As she did, I noticed that she had aged even since I had seen her last, just two years ago. The lines on her face had deepened, and she looked very tired. "You know, for me, at the time, that was not the important thing. I thought he was so handsome, so debonair, and for him to like me was so cool. Or so I thought at the time." She drifted off to her own thoughts, ignoring me as I awaited her story.

"Come on, Stephanie. What did he study?"

"Uh, something to do with butterflies. Migration, all that nonsense."

"Oh, so he was studying biology or some such?"

"Yeah, yeah. Something like that. We hopped in the sack every chance we could get. I didn't care too much about biology. That is, until I got pregnant with you. Then he seemed sooo preoccupied with his future career, and how I and you, would be in his way to success. Bastard!" She almost spat out the last word, taking another huge gulp of vodka.

"So, what happened to him? What did he do with his study of biology?"

Stephanie took a deep breath. "He left, saying he was taking on an intern position at Oregon State. It was some sort of grant project to study migration of butterflies." She looked down into her lap. "I didn't matter to him anymore, and he left. That's it. That's all I know." With that, she drained her shot glass and reached for a refill. Her face closed; the subject was over.

"So, that's it? That's all you have for me? What was his name? You have to give me that, at least."

Stephanie looked blank, then muttered, "Robert. I called him Bobby." She got up then, and stumbled over to the sofa once more, slumping down.

"I need a last name. Please, Stephanie. This is important to me." I waited; she said nothing, turning to lie down. "Come on, please. This is why I came all the way back here. To learn about my real father."

Stephanie sighed and rolled her eyes. "Oh, for heaven's sake. Why dig up the past? I can hardly remember him anyway." She turned to face the back of the sofa.

Please, Stephanie. I'm not leaving until I at least get a last name. I can't search for him without that."

"Go home. Get your adopted mom to tell you. I'm sure it's on your birth certificate or some such paper. Leave me alone and don't come back."

At that, I stomped back to the spare bedroom and grabbed my backpack. It was pointless with her. She had disappointed me my whole life. To my horror, tears streamed down my cheeks as I returned to the cramped living room, looked at the pathetic woman lying in a near stupor on the couch, and went out the front door, slamming it behind me. The flight to Bozeman had cost too much for the information I was able to glean from her. But I had a start. I walked up to the bus stop to get a ride back to the airport.

Chapter 3

I should've thought of that, I berated myself as I rode the bus to the Bozeman airport. I'd seen my birth certificate before but didn't remember or think to look at my biological father's name. I only paid attention to my mother's name—Stephanie Hoffman. I had been so focused on finding my biological mother, I overlooked the name of my father. How short sighted of me. As soon as I get back to Springville, I determined to ask Mom to pull out my birth certificate. Hopefully, with a last name, I would obtain the lead I need to find him.

"So, Mom, where is my birth certificate?" I burst into Mom's house, dragging my bag as I entered.

"What? Hi, Cassie. How was your trip to Bozeman?" Mom looked up from cleaning out Sebastian and Mandy's litter box, her plastic scoop full of soiled litter.

"Uh, uneventful as usual. I need to see the birth certificate."

"Right now? This minute?"

"Yes. Now. Sooner than later. I have to know."

Mom took a deep breath, dumping her scoop's contents into a plastic bag and tying it. "Know what, exactly? You know when you born and where. We've been over this many times." She looked weary—tired. It was nearly nine o'clock at night and she rarely stayed up past that.

"Yeah, but I never paid attention to who my real father is. His name, that is."

"Okay, but I keep important documents in the bank deposit box.

They don't open until tomorrow morning."

"Oh. Darn. Can I drive you there when they open? I need to see it as soon as possible."

"I suppose I could meet you there at nine o'clock. I have a hair appointment at ten. What's the big rush, anyway?"

"I need to find my biological dad. I have to know." I felt foolish, but at the same time, impatient and reckless.

"Cassie, sweetie, I think I remember his last name, but not sure. I think it is Harris, but it's been a long time since I really looked at that."

"Harris? So, Robert Harris? I'll meet you at the bank to be sure. It's late now. Can I just sleep over until morning?"

"Sure. Anytime." Mom looked over at me, smiling at the prospect of me staying the night with her. "The spare room is always available."

On the way down the hall to the spare bedroom, I ran into Jasmine, bending over the washing machine, loading her laundry. "Hey, Jas," I called out casually, stopping to watch her.

Jasmine looked up. "I couldn't help but overhear your conversation with Mom. So why is it so important for you to find your biological father, Cassie?" I stood with my hands folded across my chest, watching my sister, Jasmine, sort her clothes. Her long strawberry blonde hair was tied back with a scrunchie, and her makeup had long since smudged or disappeared. She wore her white bathrobe, cinched tightly at the waist.

"Well, you know. I'm not an angry teenager anymore, blaming Mom for my blind eye, but I still feel this yearning—this urge or deep need to know, to understand, who I am and who my father is. He is the key to all that I don't know about myself. I'm absolutely certain that he is the key, and I need to find him."

Jasmine looked up from the washer, pushing back her hair from her eyes, and paused her work. "At least you know now about your birth mother. Doesn't that help?"

"No! She's a raging alcoholic who never made anything of herself. And she's pasty white. I'm not any of that. Plus, I want to make a difference—be something bigger than myself. Surely, I'm more like my birth dad. He sounds like a person who achieved something worthwhile. I want to be like that."

"But our mom raised you, loved you. So did Dad. That should count for something— maybe for everything. Dad loved both of us, and I know he loved Mom, too, before he died. It's just too bad that they divorced. They loved one another very much." Jasmine's green eyes were moist as she wiped them with the back of her hand, and then bent down to add more laundry to the machine.

"Yeah, I know. But they are **your** birth parents, not mine. Tully and Sean—our parents— adopted me, you know? Then my eye got blinded in a stupid accident in the house when I was just a toddler. Both events changed my life permanently. I have to discover what I would have been if I could have known both my birth parents and not had the blinding accident. Don't you get that?" I had to know that my own stepsister understood me. It was vital to me that she understood me.

"Well," Jasmine hesitated, standing erect and turning around to speak directly to my face. I have to say, not really. Mom and Dad were all you or I ever needed growing up. How could you minimize their love and care for us? Don't you see that?" Her mouth twitched a little, like she wanted to cry, but held back. "Cassie, they loved us just the same, you and me. There was no difference between adopted or birth daughter. When I have children, I will love them equally, even if one is adopted." Jasmine looked tired. She probably had been studying all evening. She was fanatical like that about studying and always got excellent grades. I felt bad for making her talk about our growing up years.

"It's just that you are the birth child. I am not. There is a huge difference. A chasm of different emotions. I guess even you will never understand."

Jasmine glared back at me. "Gee, Cassie," she sighed. "I'm sick of your 'woe is me' attitude. Give it a rest, will you? And we've been over this before…many times, in fact."

"Okay then. Thanks for your precious time. I'll see you someday. I have to chase my dad down no matter what I find!" I stomped to the spare bedroom and slammed the door. Even doing that brought back a now distant memory when I first left home to find my birth mother. I had left then, with Mom and Dad and Jasmine standing in the doorway, helplessly watching me leave. I was only eighteen then. Maybe things hadn't really changed all that much. I was no closer to discovering my true identity now than back then. I felt a twinge of guilt speaking to Jasmine that way, in anger, but she of all people should get why I had to pursue my dream of finding the man who deserted me.

THE NEXT MORNING AT THE BANK, TULLY AND I EXAMINED THE birth certificate. There it was: "Infant girl: Casandra Louise Hoffman, born July 2, 1984, to mother, Stephanie Hoffman and father, Robert Harris." "Great. I was right. His name is Robert Harris." Mom took off her glasses, folding the document back into the safe deposit box.

That part was easy. The hard part was finding this man. Where will I start? I asked myself. I decided to begin from what Stephanie had said about him being a university student. It wasn't much to go on, but I had to pick up the thread of his existence from when he left Stephanie's life and mine began.

I said goodbye to Mom at the bank, and we each got into our separate cars. As I drove home to my apartment, I thought about this new information. Where would I begin in my search for a Robert Harris at a university from twenty some years ago? It all seemed so impossibly difficult. Then I remembered something I had nearly overlooked on the birth certificate. Also listed was place of residence for both mother and father. Stephanie's was, of course, Springville, Washington at the time of my birth. After the father's name it read, Corvallis, Oregon. That's it, of course! Robert Harris attended Oregon State at the time. Finally, I had a point of reference to begin my search, although it was an indeed remote one of ever narrowing things down to the present time.

    I had been thinking to go to a university to become a journalist—possibly get a job, eventually, as a news or feature correspondent. It was the answer to being denied enlistment into the military due to my blind eye. I would begin my application to Oregon State, and learn what I could while there about the whereabouts of my real father. I could do this, I told myself. I was still young, single, and had no roots or obligation to anyplace or anyone. I was a free woman. I smiled to myself, considering all the possibilities that lay ahead. I would and could conquer this mystery of who my birth father was and gain an adventurous career in journalism.

Chapter 4
2007

"We delight in the beauty of the butterfly, but rarely admit the changes it has gone through to achieve that beauty."
—Maya Angelou

"Uh, Dr. Jordan, thank you for agreeing to meet with me," I said, a bit nervous now that I was finally meeting the well-known former professor of the campus zoology department. After endless searching I finally discovered his whereabouts. He had retired from Oregon State University twelve years ago and was living in Lincoln City, a small town on the Oregon coast. He didn't use email, and no one knew his phone number. I obtained his mailing address at long last, and wrote him, asking if I could visit.

Before knocking on Dr. Jordan's door, I paused, sitting in the car, mentally reviewing my efforts to locate Robert Harris. I had been accepted to Oregon State and had moved to Corvallis in order to get close to where my father may have done research. I still planned to get a degree in journalism. Obtaining student loans and a couple of grants was the easy part. Studying, not so much. I wasn't a natural at schoolwork and had been working in auto repair for so long I had forgotten how difficult it could be. But my employers, the Ford Motor company, were great. They allowed me to transfer again, this time to Corvallis, and work part time while in school. I loved studying journalism, and now was close to graduating in a year.

All the while, I researched what I could to find out about Robert Harris. The school archives went back only ten years, and of course, he would have been there before that. Occasionally, I made appointments with profs who had been there a long time, to see if anyone remembered a Robert Harris who studied in the biology department, and specifically, entomology, (or the study of insects). All my searching and questioning always ended up at a dead end.

Dr. Jordan seemed to be my last hope to find out about my father's past. As I sat in front of Dr. Jordan's small cottage, I surveyed the surroundings. The bungalow set back from the gravel road, obscured by shrubs and beach grasses. The house was weather beaten and grey from years of salty air, and some of the shingles had fallen off. A ramshackle, deteriorating fence encircled the small lot. Hesitantly, I got out of my older model Jetta, and ambled up to the professor's fence, unlatching it from the inside. I knocked softly on the cottage door, its paint peeled and worn. Instantly, the door swung open. I stood face to face with Dr. Jordan, who wore a brown, buttoned sweater over a plaid shirt. He was stooped with advanced age and had balding white hair. His ice blue eyes, clouded with time, peered at me through rimless glasses that kept sliding off a bulbous nose. "Good morning," he said, greeting me with a nod and standing aside, motioning for me to enter his bungalow.

"Thank you," I stammered, not knowing quite what to say now that I was there with the professor. "Uh, my name is Casandra McMillen." I felt that I needed to confirm who I was, but he merely nodded, expecting me. "Everyone calls me Cassie." As I stepped inside, the strong aroma of vegetables cooking overpowering my nostrils.

"I'm cooking soup for dinner. I'm sure you can smell it. Sorry. Have a seat." He gestured to a worn, floral sofa. I sat down obediently, notebook and pen in hand, facing the elderly gentleman who took a frayed upholstered chair opposite. No doubt his students would have listened to his every word. He still carried himself with dignity. He leaned forward and looked at me expectantly.

I supposed that was my cue to explain why I was here. "Um, first of all, I am a student at Oregon State, studying journalism. I uh, wanted to attend there to also discover more about my biological father, Robert Harris. I, uh, hope to locate him." Suddenly, I felt childish and foolish to be disturbing this old man's tranquility with my quest. He probably remembered nothing about a Robert Harris from some twenty years ago. I was silly to have thought he would remember just another student from the past. Suddenly, I wanted to bolt out the door and drive back to Corvallis.

"Well, before we go further, Cassie, I need to be a better host. Would you care to join me for some hot tea?" His lips upturned ever so slightly. Again, he stared straight into my eyes, trying to read something there that I didn't know about. Never once did he look behind him to see what my wild blind eye refused to focus on. Even so, I felt unsettled; disturbed. The offer of tea was pleasant, however, and perhaps would give me something to do to settle my anxiety.

"Yes, that sounds very nice," I smiled, looking up. "Thank you."

He got up, walked slowly into his open kitchen, and I could hear the rattling of cups, and the sound of water boiling on the stove. Soon, he returned to the small living room bearing a tray with a teapot, two cups on saucers, two teaspoons, and cream and sugar. Very proper, I thought to myself. I liked him already. Smiling softly, he set the tea service down on the coffee table. He poured the tea, gesturing for me to take the cup nearest to my right hand, and we both sipped. It was too hot, so I added a bit of cream, and took sugar as well. I stirred the tea, and all that I could hear was the sound of the spoon inside the fine China cup, and the ticking of a grandfather clock at the far end of the room. Then he too, added cream and sugar, stirring his cup. The silence felt awkward, yet peaceful—serene. It did calm my nerves. I had hoped for a lead to find my father with this elderly man, and now that the time was here to voice my request, I didn't know how to begin.

"So, why, may I ask, do you come to me about this person, your father—Robert Harris? Why would I have useful information for your research?" His eyes, behind the rimless glasses, met mine again. The intensity disarmed me. I felt so trite—so small. His eyes seemed to envision things from long ago that I couldn't fathom. Wise. Just at that moment, out of nowhere, a huge gray cat with long fur and plume of a tail jumped up onto his lap. The cat gazed at me with enormous green eyes. It was startling.

"Oh!" I exclaimed. "I wasn't expecting that."

Dr. Jordan chuckled slightly. "Don't mind Dominican. He has to be a part of everything I do here, don't you, friend." He petted the cat on his head affectionately. I could hear the beginnings of a low rumbling purr. The purring added to the serene atmosphere. The cat set me at ease, reminding me of my cat, Nigel, from years ago.

"Uh, well, uh, I heard that you ran the biology department twenty some years ago. I thought that, maybe, uh, perhaps, you might remember something about my father, Robert Harris." I stopped, watching to see if he might light up in memory of the name. Dr. Jordan continued petting Dominican, lost in thought.

"I think I need a little more to go on. That was indeed an awfully long time ago." He set his cup down, took off his glasses, and got out a handkerchief from his back pocket to clean them. Dominican didn't budge from his lap. When he was finished cleaning the glasses, he put them back on, and replaced the cloth in his back pocket. Then he looked over at me expectantly.

"Well, uh, I don't have a lot to go on. I heard that he was given a grant to study the migration of Monarch Butterflies. And he had skin my color or darker. My biological mother is white." I chuckled nervously. I didn't understand why I felt so anxious, but my feelings were there all the same.

As if seeing me for the first time, he stared at me, then sat back. "Oh, yes, I see. You mean, African American type of fellow, right?"

I was embarrassed. "Yes, that's it, I returned, grinning sheepishly. I looked away from him, noticing for the first time a crucifix over the doorway to his home. Somehow, seeing that relaxed me. I took a deep breath and waited.

"Hmm. Let me see. That would have been roughly in the '80's, correct?"

"Right. I was born in 1984, so sometime before then."

"Okay. Early to mid '80's. We were doing many studies in entomology at the time. We got money from agricultural agencies who were trying to curb insect infestation. Hmm…. I do remember that we had the opportunity to pursue migration of the Monarchs, too. It was a side project to see how to preserve more of the population of that amazing butterfly. Yes." He raised his face to the ceiling, trying to recall something. The clock ticked on, and then chimed at the half hour. During the chimes, time seemed suspended as I anticipated his answer. Still, he contemplated silently. I continued to sip my tea, patiently hoping that something, anything, would occur to him. "I may have a couple of yearbooks saved from those years. Let me look on my bookshelves." The shelves spanned the width of the room on the far wall, which I hadn't noticed until then. He got up, the cat jumped down, and Dr. Jordan pulled a volume from the shelf, turning pages to the biology section. He scanned them quickly, turning the pages. Finally, he seemed to find what he was looking for. "Ah, yes. I remember a young man. Very industrious, bright, and enthusiastic. Extremely interested in tracing the flight of migrating Monarchs. Yes."

"You do?" I sat up brightly, anticipating more.

"Yes, I do. I think this might be the young man you were referring to, right?" He brought the book over to where I sat. Abruptly, Dominican jumped onto my lap, wanting to see the pictures in the yearbook as well.

"Oh!" I was startled again with the cat on my lap, but as I stroked him, the animal's calm inquisitiveness reassured me. Dominican's rumbling started up again, and I could feel the vibration on my lap, the yearbook poised in front of the feline. Dr. Jordan sat down on the sofa beside me, and we leafed through the pages together.

The picture's caption read, "Robert Harris, biology intern." "Yes! That's who I'm looking for! Wow! What do you know about him?" I was breathless with excitement. I couldn't help but stare at the photo—my first peek at my father. He was more handsome than I had imagined.

Dr. Jordan carried the yearbook back to his chair and took another sip of tea. "Unfortunately, not much." Dr. Jordan seemed lost in thought again, and Dominican resumed his place on the man's lap. Absently, Dr. Jordan petted the cat, running his hand from the cat's head to his lengthy tail. I slumped into the sofa, deflated. Again, I awaited any further insights. The clock ticked; the cat purred. The soup pot in the kitchen bubbled cheerily.

Five minutes or so passed. I sat on the edge of the sofa, my tea now too cold to drink. "I know the whereabouts of an old associate who may have worked with this young man. I could contact him, and if he is willing to meet with you, perhaps he could be of some help." He looked up at me dubiously with his clouded blue eyes.

"That's helpful. Please contact him," I replied, desperate for anyone, anything, to assist me to discover my birth father's whereabouts.

"I'll let you know," Dr. Jordan said, rising from his seat. The interview was over. Dominican knew it too and sauntered off to the kitchen.

As I opened the door to leave, I turned around with one more question. "Uh, where does your associate live?"

"South Padre Island, Texas."

"Oh. That's so far away." I felt defeated already. I was on a wild goose chase, with no clear end in sight. "Thank you for meeting with me, Dr. Jordan."

"If possible," Dr. Jordan smiled before continuing, "go to South Padre Island in late October."

"Why?"

"That's when you'll see the Monarchs migrating." He appeared lost in memory, as if envisioning the butterflies, and stared upwards. "Magnificent." His mind seemed to have drifted to another place, oblivious that I was still there.

PART 1
Texas

Chapter 5

2007

The tour bus stopped in front of the hostel. Beach grass waved in the soft breeze, seeming to greet those of us who got out. The wind kicked up the sand, sending it swirling into the air. I glanced around; paint was peeling off the front door, trash littered the lawn, but I could hear sea gulls cawing in the distance. It felt comforting to hear them. Waves crashed in the distance. I was here—South Padre Island. I grabbed my bag and wheeled it into the entrance, following two other young people. I had no idea what to do next, but at least, I was here at last. I had the phone number of Dr. Jordan's friend tucked into my purse and was eager to call him as soon as I could.

"Hey, Preston, are you staying here at the hostel too?" I had just met the guy on the bus but wasn't certain of his plans.

"Yeah, I guess. Can't afford a real hotel. This will have to do."

"Me too. Know anything about the island? Have you been here before?"

"Yes, and yes. I was here two years ago, and liked it so well, I decided to come back." He gave me a sideways glance, and then asked, "Want me to show you around?" He was staring at my bad eye. It never focused correctly. Some people look behind them to see what I am looking at. Sure enough, he turned quickly to see what I was staring at behind him. Of course, I really wasn't.

"Sure—I would like that. Don't bother looking to see what I'm staring at. It's just my blind eye. From a childhood accident."

"Oh, sure. No worry. I didn't notice." Preston smiled nervously, embarrassed to have fallen for the wild blind eye. All my friendships seemed to start with that. I hated it, but what could I do? Preston appeared Asian, with black hair and narrow dark eyes, along with a warm smile, which disarmed me totally. I had never really had a serious boyfriend—my blind eye always became the total focus, and that went nowhere romantically. Guys just seemed to get hung up on the darn non-focusing eye. I had my doubts that he would be any different, but time would tell.

"Okay then. Let's get checked in and we can go out for a bite. I know a cheap place not far from here. We can walk."

"Great. Just give me a few minutes to freshen up. That was a long hot bus ride," I answered, hoping to get a quick shower and change into something cooler.

"Meet you at the entrance in thirty minutes?"

"Sure." I wheeled my bag into my assigned room, which was spartan, bereft of any décor. There were two sets of bunks lining the walls, with a worn dresser on the closest wall. It was littered with assorted make up and bottles of shampoo. One young woman lounged on an upper bunk and turned to observe at me as I entered.

"The bunk below me is available," she offered, before turning her back to me.

"Okay, thanks. That'll be fine." I plopped my suitcase down on the bed, wondering where everyone kept their things. I rummaged through my bag, looking for shower supplies and a change of clothes. I didn't have much time.

"In case you're wondering, just put your suitcase under the bed. Mine is there too." As the woman turned around to say that

I caught a glimpse of her. She had red spikey hair and enormous blue eyes. "The name is Claire."

"Oh. Thanks. Mine's Cassie. Gotta grab a shower and go out, but I'll be back later." I found my toiletries and towel and took off down the hall to the large bathroom which afforded several shower stalls. At least each stall had a closing door on it. I wasn't used to public bathing.

In thirty minutes, I was standing in the hostel lobby waiting for Preston. He emerged shortly, grinning and smelling of aftershave. He wore a fresh button-down blue shirt and jeans. "Hi. Are you ready?" He asked. His hair was still wet but combed to the side.

"Sure. Let's go. I'm hungry." We set off at a brisk pace, arriving at a small pub with a nondescript sign: Bailey's Pub.

"I know it doesn't look like much, but the food is cheap and good." Preston opened the door for me, and we stepped inside the dingy eatery. It smelled of stale cigarette smoke and musty old wood. The tables were bare, worn planks of wood, which had pocked blemishes from years of use. We sat down on hard wooden chairs and picked up soiled menus. "The burgers here are great. I recommend that with a draft of beer." His eyes smiled over the menu at me, and I nodded back. A waiter approached us, with bare arms covered in tattoos, and his hair tied back in a blonde ponytail. He wore a brown apron over jeans and a t-shirt. "The lady and I will each have your burger basket and a pint." My eyebrows raised in surprise. No male had ever ordered for me before. But it was sweet and chivalrous—I liked it. "What? Isn't that what you'll have?" He looked at me, waiting.

"Uh, yes. Fine. That's it." We closed our menus, and the waiter took them, asking for our I.D.'s before disappearing behind the counter. For a few uneasy moments, neither of us spoke. I looked around in the dimly lit room, taking in the bar with wooden stools. Several people were seated there as well at tables scattered throughout.

"So," Preston broke the silence, "what brings you to the island?"

I coughed nervously before answering. Just at that moment, the waiter brought our beers. Thankfully, that gave me time to compose my answer, and I sipped on the amber liquid, buying a few more seconds. "Well, it's a long story. The short of it is, that I hope to interview someone here who may know my birth father's whereabouts."

"Whoa! That does sound complicated. But good for you. It's important to know one's family. I get that much." Preston smiled again, assuring me that he wasn't going to pry, but just await anything else I might want to share. "I thought maybe it was the sights. There is so much to enjoy here on the island. I love it."

"Plus," I ventured, emboldened by his interest, "I hope to see migrating or overwintering Monarch Butterflies while I'm here. Supposedly they come through here on their way to Mexico during late October."

"My, my, my. Aren't you full of surprises? I took you for a regular tourist. Are you a university student studying insects or something?" He asked with an amused smile but seemed sincere.

"No, I study journalism. But my father studied them as a student years ago. I hope to talk to his friend who may still live here. Maybe he will have information as to where my father went. I know it's a long shot. But it's all I have at this point." I felt a bit foolish, realizing it sounded so farfetched out loud. I looked at Preston to see how he took it.

"Um hm, uh hm," he said, nodding. He leaned forward from across the table. "Sounds a bit much, but interesting at the same time. I wish you luck with that. Let me know what you come up with."

"Have you seen the butterflies here?"

"No, but I always come for the typical beach scene. You know, chicks and all that," he teased. I couldn't tell if he was serious or not. "But hey. If you see some, let me know. We could go there together, right?"

"Sure. I'll find out more when and if I meet this old friend of my father's." At that, I stared into my nearly empty glass of beer.

Preston noticed, and signaled the waiter. "We'll each have another pint." Then he turned back to me. "Tell me more about yourself." He smiled so encouragingly that I told him all about myself, on the condition that he would do the same.

"So, Preston, tell me about you, now," I asked, after going through my story of being adopted, the accident with my eye as a toddler, and leaving home at eighteen to meet my biological mom. I even included how my adoptive parents divorced, and later my stepfather dying of a heart attack. I looked at Preston over my almost empty glass and waited for him to speak.

"Well, it's your average run-of-the-mill story about a Chinese American boy growing up in Frisco." He chuckled a little, realizing the joke was on him. So, my Chinese American family has lived in San Francisco for five generations."

"Whoa! Stop a moment." I sat back in my chair, incredulous. "Are you serious? I can't even trace my family back even one generation yet. I'm still searching. Amazing! Must be nice. Do you have family records that go back that far?"

"Sure. I know from records at the courthouse, which my grandfather made copies of, that our family arrived by ship back in the 1800's. Even know the name of the ship that they came over in. You know, they came for jobs on the railroad construction."

"I am so envious. That's wonderful that you know all of that about your family roots."

"Yeah, but most people aren't impressed. You know, racial stigma and all that." He grinned sheepishly, setting down his empty glass.

"I can only imagine what my roots are like if I could go back five generations. Not very impressive for African American beginnings either. But I hope I can find out all about my ancestors."

"Sure. I hope you can. Like I said already, family is important." He smiled encouragingly, signaling the waiter who walked past. "Another one, Cassie?"

"No, two is plenty for me. But go ahead. I want you to tell me more about yourself."

He ordered another pint and continued to share more about himself. I found out that Preston graduated a year ago from the University of Southern Cal with a bachelor's in English literature and was now twenty-three. Supposedly, he loved coming to the island to get inspired to write his great Chinese American novel and hoped one day to become famous. I scoffed at that, but at least, he had dreams. I, too, had dreams, centered around finding my dad. We finished after a couple of hours and walked back to the hostel and said our goodnights, with the promise to meet up the next day to look around the island.

Chapter 6

Aside from my senior prom, which was a "pity" date, from my best friend's cousin, I had never dated anyone. I wasn't going to count grabbing a burger with Preston, since we were just eating a meal out of necessity, and each of us paid for our own. He seemed to be a great guy, sincere and all that, but I felt he was more like a brother.

After we finished our burgers and beer, we ambled back to the hostel, chatting amicably. As we entered the hostel, Claire was leaving our room. "Hey, girlfriend, who is this?" Claire flashed Preston a wide grin and paused in the hallway.

"Preston Chang," he interjected for me. I was still in shock at her calling me "girlfriend' already. I hung back as they shook hands.

"Claire Middleton," she returned. I didn't even know her last name yet, so this was fortuitous. I wouldn't have to ask her. "How long are you here on the island?"

"Oh, at least a couple of weeks. I come here every year. Love it."

"Well, don't be a stranger. Let's do some stuff while we're all here. Right Cassie?" Claire addressed me at last.

I nodded my head enthusiastically. "Yes, certainly! Let's do stuff." I had no idea what that meant, or where we could go. I was a totally new tourist here.

Preston picked up on that and rescued me. "I know of a dolphin rescue place. They give tours and all that. Let's go there tomorrow, if you are both available?" He looked from me to Claire.

"Sounds great! Let's go! Right, Cassie?"

"Sure! What time?"

"Let's go late morning, say, eleven?" Preston looked at us again. "Unless that's too early?" We all agreed it was fine, and I said goodnight to Preston and set foot into my room.

The next morning, I attempted to call my contact from Dr. Jordan, a man named Guy Collins. He didn't answer so I left a message and went down to the beach, wearing a swimsuit, and carrying a book and a beach towel. The wind picked up, so it seemed too brisk to go for a swim. I lounged on the towel, reading, but it felt too cold even for that. As I got up, I brushed the sand off, and prepared to trudge back to the hostel. At that moment, a man whom I surmised to be around thirty, approached. "Hi. You must be new here. The name is Ramon," he said, extending his hand. His eyes took me in, with my frizzy Afro hair, two-piece green swimsuit, and of course, the one eye that refused to focus. He automatically glanced behind, to see what I was looking at. Immediately, I was embarrassed, not only for the eye, but the fact that he caught me out here like a newbie, thinking I could swim on a cool October morning. The beach was empty except for the two of us.

"Uh, hello. I'm Cassie. Yes, I just got here yesterday, and thought I could come out here and swim. Silly of me for sure."

"Oh, not really. You'd be surprised at how many locals swim here this time of year. It's just a little early in the day for them." He smiled reassuringly, his brown eyes sparkling and warm. He was about six inches shorter than I, stocky but well built, with dark brown hair that touched his shoulders. He wore faded cutoff jeans with holes and a white T shirt. I observed strong biceps where the shirt sleeves ended. "Mind if I sit down with you for a few minutes?"

"Uh, suit yourself. I'm going to be here only a couple minutes more. It's too windy out here." I felt a sense of foreboding for some reason. I didn't want to linger with a total stranger out on the beach alone. "In fact, I think I'll go back now. I'm freezing." I feigned a little shiver to emphasize my statement, and stood up, gathering up the towel and shaking it, and then clutched onto my book. I set off at a trot, anxious now to return to the safety of the hostel, aware that Ramon would probably follow me.

"Sure. No worry. I'll chat with you as we walk." He easily caught up with me as we trekked through the loose sand. At one point, his thigh brushed mine, he was so close. I felt weird and a little apprehensive. Who was this man to assume he could just sidle up beside me like we were old buddies? "So, uh, Cassie, is it? What do you say we meet up tonight at this new pub I know down the beach about a half mile, called Beach Bums? It's easy to find. I'll be there around eight if you want to join me for a pint." I said nothing, striding purposefully, giving myself time to think of my answer.

"Well, maybe. I think my roommate and I may be going out tonight. I'll check with her to see if she wants to go there." In my mind, I was thinking I needed backup for this one. I hoped she would go along with the ruse.

"Okay, sure. Maybe I'll see you." I had arrived at my hostel and had already veered off to the entrance.

"Sure." I kept my head down, not wanting to look up at him. I raced to my room, hoping that Claire was there. Sometimes she went out, but I never knew when. I unlocked the door and swung it open. Claire was laying out clothes to put on for the day and glanced back at me as I entered.

"My, aren't you an early bird today," she said, almost as more of a complaint than a comment.

"Yeah, I suppose I am. Wanted to catch some fresh air at the beach this morning. It's been a long time since I got to lie out on the sand."

Claire sat up, suddenly alert. "Well, just be careful. It's not good to be alone around here at odd hours. Know what I mean?" She looked at me carefully, to see if I understood.

"Right. In fact, I did run into someone out there. No one else was out yet." I hesitated to share more and waited for her response.

"Um hm. Like I said."

"Okay. So, here's the deal. This guy, Ramon, asked me to meet him tonight at Beach Bums at eight. I told him that you and I were going out and wasn't sure, but maybe… uh, that you would go with me." I felt silly now. Who was I to presume on Claire? I barely knew her. "Sooo, what do you say?" I twisted my frizz of hair that had escaped the rest of the mass of curls, nervously watching her reaction.

Claire shrugged her shoulders. "Why not? Nothing else better to do at eight tonight. Sure. I'll go. Is he cute? Did you ask if he had a friend?" She leaned forward, a bit excited at the prospect.

"Uh, he didn't say. But I told him you might be coming, so who knows? Thanks a lot, Claire. I owe you."

"Sure, no prob. Let's go over our wardrobes and figure out what to wear for this tonight. But, say. What about that other guy I saw you with? Preston, isn't it?" She paused by the closet, looking at me quizzically with her enormous aqua colored eyes. Her red hair still stood spiked up, even though she had just gotten out of bed.

Oh, him. He's a really nice person. More like just a friend type. Know what I mean?"

Claire shrugged in indifference. "Sure. Just wondering. Let's look at the clothes selections now." We had fun for the next twenty minutes, going over our wardrobe selections for the evening outing. At least, we were fast becoming friends. I liked that prospect. I hoped this Ramon took the bait and brought a friend for Claire.

Soon, it was time for our outing with Preston to the dolphin rescue center. We arrived there in no time, since the island was a small place. As we toured and watched the dolphins, each of us got to give a dolphin a fish to eat. We laughed and enjoyed the time, which ended too soon. As we strolled back to the hostel, we made plans for the next day to go to the sea turtle rescue, a place not far from the hostel. All the while, I kept mulling over the possibilities that lay in store that evening with Ramon. I felt nervous but also curious. My first real date.

Chapter 7

Claire selected a short denim skirt with holes in the front and a low slinging black tunic top. She finished it off with heels— three-inch black sandals. Her red hair stood on end at extreme angles, aided by a stiff gel. She flashed me a grin as we entered the dimly lit, smoke-filled interior of Beach Bums. I ended up wearing my best black jeans with a violet button down top, and black flats. I had decided on understatement instead of flashy and attempted to get my hair to behave in its natural, soft frizz. We created a contrast—Claire, with ivory white complexion and spikey red hair, and me, ebony skinned and frizzy black tresses, as we swung open the heavy wooden door, all heads swiveling around to greet us with stares. Claire led the way, tall and lithe, clomping noisily on the hard floor in her platform heels. I nudged her when I glanced over and noticed Ramon sitting at a table on a tall stool. Across from him sat another man about his age, also with dark hair and eyes. Claire noticed the friend, turning to give me the look as if to say, "That's what I'm talking about." I was grateful that Ramon came through with a date for Claire. So far, so good.

The two men stood up to introduce themselves. Fortunately, they seemed to have some manners. "Hi Cassie. So, who's your friend?" Ramon stared at Claire, obviously enjoying gawking at her. Her blouse revealed a little cleavage, and he couldn't seem to take his eyes off it.

"Well, this is Claire. Claire, Ramon," I finished, nodding to him, and waiting for the next intro.

"I'm Angel," the new man interjected, not waiting for Ramon. He reached out for a handshake. "So, Claire, are you new to the island?" He took her in appreciatively with his gaze.

"No, not so much. I've been here many times. Like my second home," she sniffed, raising her chin. Claire hooded her eyes, looking past Angel as if to dismiss him a bit. I could see that she liked playing hard to get.

He smiled and just winked at her, inviting us to sit by pulling up two more stools. "Here. Sit. We'll get our server. "So, what brings you back to the island?" He peered down her blouse, not even trying to hide his interest. I felt bile rise up in my throat. How could I have thought that she would want to come with me? On the other hand, I was totally new at this. She seemed much more knowledgeable in this department of meeting guys at bars. Casually, she crossed her right leg over her left, and her skirt went up even higher. Angel looked on in undisguised lust.

"Oh, the weather. I like it here," was all Claire would say. I fiddled with my napkin, wondering where this was going. Just then, the server appeared, a trim young woman with black fake lashes and long, bleach blonde hair.

"What'll you have?" the waitress, named Tina according to her name badge, asked Claire, moving close to her side.

"A margarita is fine." Tina looked over at me, waiting.

"Uh, I'll have the same," I stammered, even though I had never had a margarita before. I felt so uncomfortable here, I wasn't sure what to order or what to do. Ramon just grinned reassuringly in my direction. I tried to relax on the stool, but it was a challenge. Maybe once the drinks arrived, it would help. The two men finished their first drinks and ordered refills. They were drinking stout beers. Claire downed the remainder of her drink and then motioned to me with her eyes that she wanted me to accompany her to the ladies' room.

Most of my drink was still in the glass, but I left it. We got up and excused ourselves, and I followed Claire, her hips swinging as she clomped off to the restroom.

"So, what's up? What do you think?" I asked her as we entered the safety of the restroom.

"What I think is that Angel is your typical, sleezy bar pick-up. I can handle that—at least for one night. And you?" Claire met my gaze.

"Well, I'm not sure. I haven't had much experience at this. I went out with Preston as a friend. That's been about it in the dating department. My blind eye puts men off."

"Oh, I wouldn't be so sure. It looks like Ramon isn't put off. But just be careful. You know what I mean? Get to know him first. I know men. They can be animals."

"Thanks, Claire." Claire snapped her handbag shut after touching up her bright red lipstick, and we made our way back through the murky room, a Guns and Roses number blaring from speakers. I forgot to bring my lipstick, so I did nothing but follow her lead back. The drink was still waiting for me there, and I decided to drink it down, hoping that it would help with my inhibitions at this whole new thing. As I took the last few sips, Ramon smiled at me, and touched my leg under the table. I didn't like that, and drew away a bit, shifting my leg in the other direction. When Claire and Angel ordered another round of drinks, Ramon motioned to me with a nod to join him on a sofa in a dark corner of the bar. Claire saw the signal and gave me a look that clearly said to be careful. Cautiously, I jumped down from the stool and followed him. I sat down on the edge of the sofa, but Ramon wrapped his arm around me to draw me close.

"I won't bite, Cassie. Let's just sit and enjoy the music." I felt nervous; what was happening? "Are you okay? Want another drink?" Ramon had his right arm around me and with his left hand, caressed my hair, and then my cheek and then ear lobe. "Your hair is so soft. So is your skin," he murmured into my ear.

"Uh, no, I'm fine. Just not used to another person touching me so soon after meeting him." A wave of panic rose from my gut but was soon replaced by a reckless urge to just enjoy the moment.

"Um hmm. That's okay. No worries." He continued to stroke my face, and then leaning in, put his tongue in my ear. My brain said to recoil, but my body begged for more. I responded by moving in closer to him, touching his thigh. Soon, I wanted to go higher with my touch, to his crotch. Ramon just smiled, and took my hand, leading me out of the bar. Claire glanced over at me in horror, getting up from her seat, acting as if she was going to object or block me from leaving. I averted my eyes, aiming uncertainly for the door's exit. "I know a place where we can have privacy, Cassie. Just let me lead the way." Ramon spoke softly into my ear, holding me close.

Obediently, I accompanied him—I felt helpless to do otherwise. I didn't even protest—how was that possible? By now, my legs felt wobbly, and my desire for him was so strong, I thought I would go crazy until we reached this secret place he mentioned. What was happening to me? I felt powerless at Ramon's touch as he guided me down the sidewalk. All I knew was that I had an overpowering desire to have sex with him. Soon, we were walking down a small trail to the dunes. He pulled me into a sheltering cover of tall grasses and down onto the sand. He began unzipping my jeans, and by then, he was on top of me. I didn't even object. It was what my body was craving, but my mind was in a fog.

When it was over, I just cried. How did this happen to me? Why did I feel so confused? Ramon just left me there, like an old used rag, disappearing into the dark. I rezipped and rebuttoned as best I could, and by the light of the moon, stumbled back up the path to the hostel, and found my room. I threw myself onto my bed, sobbing quietly. Claire was already asleep, since by then it was past one in the morning.

Chapter 8

Claire sat on the bed in her Disney Minnie Mouse pajamas with me the next morning. I was still dressed from last night; my violet top partially buttoned the wrong way. Groggy from the drug, I still didn't fully comprehend what she was saying. "So, you were raped, Cassie. Date raped with a date rape drug."

"What do you mean? I really wanted him to do it to me."

"Exactly. That's how the drug works. That way, the guy gets off the rape charge, and you both have a good time. For the moment." Claire gently took my hand. "So sorry, kiddo. I warned you, but somehow he slipped you something like ecstasy, probably in your drink."

Suddenly, I remembered. "Yes. You and I went to the restroom, and I had more margarita left in my glass. You had drunk all of yours."

Claire inhaled sharply. "Oh, no. Right! So sorry. I always make it a habit to down my drink before I leave a table with a new date. I forgot to tell you that precaution." She inspected me sadly. I saw my reflection in the mirror: smeared makeup, hair sticking out at odd angles, and blouse askew. I looked down to my jeans, which were dirty and bloodstained.

"Did it ever happen to you?" I asked, shame overcoming me. I felt such a fool.

Claire hesitated. "Yes, actually it did. That's how I know. Sooo sorry, girlfriend," she continued, shaking her head in regret and sorrow. "I should have warned you of that one. It's an old trick some sons of bitches use. What a way for you to find out!" Claire's eyes flamed in anger. "You were a virgin, too, am I right?"

"Yes," I admitted slowly. "Twenty-three and a virgin, yes. Like I said, I'm pretty inexperienced in the world of dating. I've spent my life working and going to school and searching for my bio parents. Some life, huh?" I started sobbing, holding onto her hand tightly.

"Oh, honey, don't worry. You're young. You will recover from this." Claire seemed so experienced, so wise in the ways of men. In actuality, she was only two years my senior. I clung to her as if she were a life preserver and wept uncontrollably, my head leaning onto her shoulder. Claire took me in her arms, patting me on the back, comforting me like a mother hen gathering her chick into her protective wings. There were no more words to be said about it. I felt humiliated and heartbroken. My introduction to sex had happened in a strange place, with a strange man, and then he took advantage of me. I cried and cried, Claire patiently holding me against her chest until the tears were silent and eyes parched.

CLAIRE TRIED TO TALK ME INTO CALLING THE POLICE. I WAS determined to leave that morning, so I said no. I didn't want to go through the medical examination and filling out a police report—I just wanted to be rid of the place. I dressed and after hugging Claire goodbye and exchanging phone numbers with her, I took the first bus heading back to the airport. I didn't say goodbye to Preston; shame fretted at my mind, and I just couldn't face him. I didn't know what to say without risking a teary break down. Before leaving, I called to book a last-minute flight back to Portland. From there, I would catch a shuttle to Corvallis, where my apartment was near the university.

As the plane carried me home, I watched out the window from my seat. I thought about Dr. Jordan's friend, Guy, and wished I had been able to meet him and witness the wondrous migrating Monarchs. The butterflies would have to wait until a future October, as well as my discovering the whereabouts of my father. It was truly a huge personal setback for me. The sadness of it all caught in my throat. When the flight attendant asked what I would like to drink, I ordered a hot tea, futilely hoping to settle my rising grief. It kept resurfacing, taunting, and accusing me as the miles raced by.

That first night at home, I cried myself to sleep. I arose from a fitful, restless night with swollen eyes, but visited the school nurse for an examination to make sure I was okay physically. Nothing would ease my emotional state. The bleeding still hadn't stopped, but the nurse reassured me I would be okay. Nothing could fix the damage to my psyche, however. I felt permanently scarred. My trust was obliterated, and I would always carry the shame.

Rain
(Fall)

The clouds release their contents,

Dark, menacing, and threatening,
as they pelt down

Drops of moisture onto the parched ground,

Longing to quench its thirst,

To revitalize green shoots once more,
after the long drought of summer.

Once considered ominous, now the hush
of mists descends upon the city,

A comfort to withered grasses and trees, who reach
up to slake their yearning, though warm weather
buffs mourn the inevitable torrents.

For nature, however, a welcome sign of life restored.

The sun hides its face as the days become shorter.

We huddle indoors, listening to the patter
on leaves and roof tops.

As the dreary days commence.

Chapter 9
November 2007

For a week, I didn't let my family know that I had returned ahead of time from South Padre Island. I resumed classes and asked my boss if I could go back to work earlier than I had originally requested. Finally, one morning before class, Jasmine called me to see what I was up to. I tried to pretend that nothing was out of the ordinary—that I had I just finished up my vacation early. "So, did you see the butterflies?" Jasmine asked.

"Well, no. I need to go back next October. Something came up and I didn't meet Dr. Jordan's friend." I sniffed, hoping to sound casual, my hand gripping a cup of coffee. I took a sip, trying to think of what to say next.

"Well, how will it help to go back another time? What if you run into a snag again, and still don't get a lead on your dad? What then?" Jasmine persisted in her know-it-all, common sense tone she always used on me.

"Oh, it won't happen next time, believe me," I emphasized a little too heavily.

"How do you know? Maybe it will."

"Absolutely it won't. I'll make sure of that," I thought, my throat constricting a little at the thought of Ramon and what he had done to me.

Jasmine picked up on my words getting caught in my throat. "What happened, exactly, Cassie? Are you okay?" I detected her concern now instead of criticism.

"Oh, nothing, really. I'm fine. I just didn't get to see this person named Guy Collins like I had planned. No big deal. I'll go back another time."

"Kind of expensive to keep making trips there, isn't it? It's so far out of the way compared to most places. Isn't it at the tip of Texas or somewhere?" Jasmine kept prodding, trying to get me to say more. I wasn't ready for more. Maybe never would be.

"Yeah, but I'll just work extra hours to earn enough to go back. No worries. Say, did Mom ask you to call to try to get information out of me?" I was suspicious. She was poking around too much for my comfort.

"Yes and no. I told her I was going to call you, and she wanted me to find out why you came back early."

Chapter 10
Spring 2008

"Nature's message was always there and for us to see. It was written on the wings of butterflies."

—Kjell B. Sandved

I buried myself in my schoolwork and my job. The shame of what had happened on the island haunted me by night as I attempted to sleep. Nightmares followed me constantly, and I was restless and tormented, always reliving the night of my rape. I finally made an appointment with my doctor to get something to help me sleep for my tortured mind. I wasn't sure how I would ever face going back to South Padre Island; I feared running into Ramon. I avoided my mom and Jasmine as much as I dared and drove up to Springville only one time. I slept a lot, and stayed aloof, not talking to them much. So far, they hadn't let on that they could tell that something was wrong.

Dr. Jordan called to ask if I had located my father. I simply replied that the trip didn't lead to any big discovery; I just couldn't tell him what had really happened. Six months after my trip to the island, he invited me for a soup lunch with him and Dominican at his beach home. It sounded like a nice break from my studies. For spring break, I booked a hotel in the same town where he lived, in Lincoln City, and headed over to the coast.

As the grandfather clock ticked in the living room corner and the soup bubbled on the kitchen stove, the aroma of vegetables cooking reminded me that I was hungry. I had already lost ten pounds since my return from the island. Food just didn't appeal to me with my internal anxiety. Dr. Jordan studied my face intently, seeming to comprehend it all. Dominican remembered me and jumped onto my lap. I petted his luxurious long, gray fur, staring down at him while I could feel Dr. Jordan's cloudy blue eyes looking at me for answers, yet he asked no questions. Yet. Dominican purred loudly, seeming to hit the same rhythm as the clock ticking. I relaxed, despite myself and my inner turmoil.

"You know, Cassie, you can tell me anything. I have only Dominican to share with, and he doesn't care what I say. He knows how to keep things to himself," he chuckled, enjoying his own little joke. I continued to stroke Dominican, maybe a bit too hard, as the cat gently bit at my hand to slow my petting down. Then I felt tears behind my eyes; I tried to brush them away, but one drop fell on Dominican, who continued to rumble his low purr.

"I'm not certain that I can, Dr. Jordan. It's still very painful—and humiliating."

"Have you told anyone what happened? Anyone?" He stared at me with such kindness and compassion, I cried even more.

"Only the one female friend I made on the island, and —my doctor."

At the mention of the word "doctor," Dr. Jordan stood, his lips forming a straight line, seeming to reveal that he comprehended more than I had told him. "I'll make us some tea and we can talk a bit more while the soup simmers. Is that alright with you?" His gentle question created more tears, so I nodded my consent, and he limped into the kitchen to put on the water for tea. I hadn't noticed his limp the first time I met him. He seemed even more bent over and slower moving than I remembered. Of course, at that time, all I could think about was finding my real father. I sat on the worn, floral sofa in the silence of the living room, continuing to stroke Dominican until he got tired of it, and jumped down to join Dr. Jordan in the kitchen. The clock chiming on the quarter hour was my only company for a few minutes. Dr. Jordan remained in the kitchen until the water boiled, and he brought in a tray with his teapot and cups, Dominican trailing behind him.

Dr. Jordan poured the tea, motioning for me to use the sugar and creamer he had placed on the tray. I took both, stirring longer than necessary. Dr. Jordan did the same. Dominican sat beside me on the sofa this time, seeming to understand the need for more space during tea drinking. Finally, I lifted the cup to my lips. "Ooo, too hot!" I exclaimed, setting the cup down onto my saucer. Dr. Jordan simply nodded, placing his cup and saucer onto the coffee table coaster to cool. Silence reigned for at least two more minutes as the clock marked the passing of time. I was afraid to say anything; the shame and tears threatened to take over. Dr. Jordan understood, and said nothing. I could sense that the tears were on the verge of forming and so did he.

Finally, "Something unpleasant occurred regarding a young man, am I correct?" He said it gently, nearly inaudibly, but I heard him.

"Yes," I whispered. "I'm so ashamed." Drops of moisture fell from my eyes and onto my lap. I felt the choking sensation in my throat as it constricted in anguish.

"I'm so sorry this happened to you. Give it some time; you were wounded, but you will heal. Then you will be wiser and stronger." He placed his hand on my knee, his simple gesture of caring overcoming me with more tears.

"I—I don't know if I can ever go back there. I need to, but I'm afraid. Afraid I will see this—this man. What will I do?" I implored him as a child would, seeking strength and reassurance. I glanced up on the wall above the entrance to the kitchen. There, the simple crucifix was still in place, seeming to signal to me that everything would one day be okay.

"When you are ready, you will return. You will go with a singular purpose—to talk to my friend, Guy, about your father, and… you will witness the wondrous migration of the Monarchs. That alone will change your life. Trust me." Dr Jordan smiled serenely, lifting his eyes to the ceiling, recalling the image of the migrating butterflies. "Wait to go during the month of October, whether it be this year or another. But don't wait too long. Each year there seem to be fewer of them. Plus, there is your quest to find your father. Go." At that, Dr. Jordan took my hand in his, grasping it firmly. I looked down, tracing the veins of his hand with my finger. I simply nodded, taking in all that he had just said. "Now, let's go into the kitchen and prepare to eat our lunch."

I followed Dr. Jordan and Dominican into the small, compact kitchen. He motioned for me to sit at his table, and then proceeded to ladle up two bowls of steaming vegetable soup. I saw the circles of bright orange carrots and soft, creamy chunks of potato floating in the steamy broth. He placed the bowls on a plate, and on each one, a slab of thick white bread, already buttered. Dr. Jordan sat down then, and bowing his head, offered a simple prayer. I was glad I hadn't taken a bite yet of the yummy looking bread. Nervously, I bowed my head too. He looked up at me, and taking up his spoon, gestured for me to do the same. Dominican went over to a corner of the kitchen where his cat bowl held dry food and crunched away on his cat lunch as well. Neither of us said much, but toward the end of the meal, Dr. Jordan cleared his throat.

"Heh, heh. Dominican always joins me for meals." he said, watching Dominican. "Uh, Cassie. There was another reason that I invited you for lunch today. I have something to ask you." He set his spoon down and took a sip of water. "Is that okay with you if I ask you something?"

"Uh, sure, Dr. Jordan. Anything." I couldn't imagine what he wanted to ask, and paused in my eating, swallowing what was already in my mouth. I took a drink of water too and waited.

"I have no close relatives around. If I am no longer able to care for Dominican someday, will you take care of him? Treat him as your own cat?" Dr. Jordan turned to me, his face clearly worried and anguished. The wrinkles around his lips and eyes were more pronounced. It was clear that this idea was weighing heavily on his mind. "I don't want him to go to a shelter—or something worse." His eyes were pleading with me.

"Uh, of course, Dr. Jordan. Yes, I will take Dominican." At his name, Dominican sidled up to me, and I reached down to pat him on the head. Relief surged in my mind as I had conjured up other questions Dr. Jordan might have asked me. I was flattered at the request, realizing that Dr. Jordan would want someone special to whom he could entrust his beloved cat. "I would be honored to take him as my own. But you are strong, yet. You shouldn't worry about that."

"Well, Cassie, I appreciate that. But I am becoming feebler and must plan for things. Dominican is my life now. When this happens,

I will let you know. For now, you must think of your career future, and discovering your father's whereabouts. Thank you for saying yes. Just in case, I will write you down in my important papers. In case I'm too sick to call you."

This time when I left Dr. Jordan, I gave him a hug, which he gratefully returned. More tears fell onto my cheeks as I walked away. It was hard to leave him and Dominican, but I promised to return before too much time had slipped by.

Chapter 11
June 2008

"Hey, girlfriend. Why haven't you called?" I heard the perky voice of Claire on my phone. I hadn't even had time for coffee yet and rubbed my eyes to get awake. I glanced at the clock; it was only six in the morning. I had to get ready for work soon, but it was nice that she called me before I left.

"Well, uh, I've been busy, what with work and finishing up my degree. Sorry," I finished, sounding a bit lame even to my sleepy ears.

Claire chuckled. "Glad to hear that you are busy. That's the best therapy. So, when are you returning to the island? I'll arrange to meet up with you then. My schedule at the office is fairly flexible. I just have to put in for time off." Claire paused, then continued. "Say, is it okay for me to give Preston your number? He called me and asked for it. He's wondering why you left the island in such a rush. I didn't say anything of course."

Dr. Jordan and Claire were right, I thought to myself as I held the phone, listening to Claire babble on about her latest boyfriend. I needed to plan to return to the island the following October. I had been going over it all in my mind as to why finding my father was so important to me. I had gone over my reasons. Finding my real mother was a huge disappointment. What if he was a letdown as well? How would I feel then? Would it spiral me down into a depression, convinced that I was a worthless human being all along, and never wanted by my parents? That I was just a mistake? Was the search worth the risk of that disillusionment? Plus, I reasoned, living with the adopted family had not been so bad, right? At least I had someone to go "home" to occasionally, and a sister that liked me most of the time.

Yet, it wasn't enough. I needed the full picture of my origins; I had to find out who I really was. Maybe my natural father was the missing puzzle piece to my life, so I had to try to find him. Maybe, just maybe, there was another explanation that Stephanie wasn't telling me about their relationship. Perhaps he was a successful, intelligent man. I had to find out.

My throat tightened a bit, remembering the reason why I had departed the island in such a hurry. Claire had just asked me a question. I heard the pause, and I snapped back to reality. "Sorry, what did you say?"

"I asked if you didn't mind if I gave Preston your number. And I didn't say anything to him about why you left."

"Yeah, right. I knew you wouldn't say anything. Sure, it's okay to give Preston my number. I'll think of something to say to him when he calls as to why I disappeared so abruptly. Say, let me start some coffee. Hang on a moment." I started the coffee brewer and came back to the phone. "Okay. Where were we?"

"Well, back on the island, I hope. When shall we plan for it this time? I can let Preston know, too. He wants to hang out with us."

I tittered a little out loud. "Why does he want that?"

"We're friends, girlfriend. Why not?"

"I'll see what I can do about going and get back to you. It has to be in October, for the Monarch migration."

Claire sighed. "All right. I get it. That's what brought you there in the first place, right?"

"Yes, of course. I have to meet up with this old friend of my father's, and he lives there on the island in order to observe and record the annual migration. I need to arrange that, too. And call Dr. Jordan." My list of to-dos seemed to be growing.

"Who's Dr. Jordan?" Claire sounded bored already. And I had to get dressed for work anyway.

"I'll tell you more later. Gotta run." My coffee was ready, and I took out a mug from the cabinet and poured a cup, glancing again at the clock on the microwave. I barely had time to get dressed for work and grabbed a banana on the way out the door.

Later, that evening, Preston called. "Hey, Cass. Are we meeting up on the island in October? I talked to Claire, and she said as much."

"Nice to hear from you, Preston. Yeah, I'm ready for a vacation again." At least, I am ready as far as taking time off was concerned. I don't know about emotionally. "Let's set a time to meet there soon. I'll send some dates to you and Claire and see what works." As we chatted, I sensed that he was hoping for more than a reacquaintance of a friendship. I hoped that I wasn't leading him on—I just felt like he was the brother I never had. He seemed safe; comfortable. I wanted to keep our relationship that way.

I HAD COMPLETED MY DEGREE THAT SPRING WHILE WORKING at the car dealership. At the same time, I applied for several correspondent positions. I wanted to use my journalism degree by reporting for news outlets. I soon discovered that it was indeed an extremely competitive field, and I would have to start at the bottom, locally. I found that even that was difficult to break into. So, I just asked for more hours at my mechanic job.

The summer rushed by in a blur, with me under the hood of cars forty plus hours a week. I had little time for anything else, including seeing my mother, Tully, and sister, Jasmine. They still lived in Springville, but I continued renting my university apartment in Corvallis. In a way, aside from the fact that the job kept me in Corvallis, it was easier to avoid them. The wound from my rape experience was still very raw; embarrassment and humiliation constantly pricking the edges of my consciousness.

No prospects of a correspondent position arose, no matter how many resumes I sent out. I just worked that much harder at Ford, exhausted every night from sheer labor. It was good therapy— until I opened the letter late one afternoon in late August. The letter was from a Sarah Guthrow, from a town in Washington state, just outside Springville. I nearly tossed the letter, assuming it was junk mail, until I read, "I regret to inform you that my older sister, Stephanie Hoffman, died July 2 from heart failure. She died alone in her rented home in Bozeman. A neighbor found her in her unlocked home, but she had already passed away, presumably the day or so before."

Heart failure from her alcoholism, no doubt. The thought had never occurred to me regarding Stephanie. I felt numb; my hand gripped the letter as my eye took in the rest of the words on the page. Sarah left a phone number, encouraging me to contact her as soon as I received the message. So, I called her. After introducing myself, Sarah said, "Yes, your mother, Stephanie Hoffman, died a month ago of heart failure.

"What are you saying? Who are you and how do you know that I'm her biological daughter? She wanted nothing to do with me, ever." I felt the familiar disappointment, the rejection, lurking at the back of my mind.

"My name is Sarah Guthrow, like I said. I am Stephanie's younger sister. We rarely kept in touch, but she told me about you. Also, I am her executor as such. She had a will, believe it or not."

This was just too much to process. I sat down on a kitchen chair, one hand on the phone, and the other lay on my lap, trembling. What fresh horrible news was this? Where was it leading? I said nothing, just continued holding onto the phone, my knuckles turning white from the grip. I switched hands.

"Stephanie loved you very much. She left a letter with the will, mentioning her love for you over and over. She wanted so much for you to be successful, to grow up to be a strong, young woman with many more opportunities than she could ever give you."

"Oh, right. I saw how much she loved me. She cast me aside me at birth and from that moment on," I complained bitterly. "She hated the very sight of me the few times I visited her."

"Not true. Can we meet and go over all of this? You can read the letter and will for yourself. She left her few possessions to you. The manufactured home was a rental, so my son and I emptied out her possessions. There wasn't much of value, but what there is, belongs to you now. It's stored in my garage."

"I hope you got rid of all of her worn out furniture," I said sarcastically. "I wouldn't touch that nasty stuff. Plus, I don't need any threadbare items." I snorted at my lame attempt at humor, while Sarah waited quietly and patiently.

"Nooo," she answered slowly. "We left them with the house. We learned that the trailer was rented as a furnished home. What we took are her personal effects. We donated all of her clothing."

"Thank goodness. I don't want to have to go through all that garbage." I knew I was being mean, but I couldn't help myself. Look what she had done to me by forsaking me my entire life. What mother does that?

I agreed to drive up that coming Saturday and meet with Sarah at her house. I could also see my mom and sister since she lived just a few miles from them. At least, I would have Stephanie's demise to talk about, and stay away from the topic of my traumatic dating experience.

Chapter 12

I stopped once on the long drive to Kent to get coffee and a sandwich, and then pushed on. The trip took about six hours, but there would be time enough for resting later, at Mom's. When I pulled up to Sarah Guthrow's house it was around two in the afternoon that Saturday. The house was a one-level ranch style, nestled among larger, two level homes on a dead-end street. Overgrown bushes flanked each side of the house. Weeds sprouted boldly in the crevices of the sidewalk leading up to the steps. Not very welcoming. I hesitantly got out of my car, set the alarm, and ambled up the walk slowly. I wished at this point that we had agreed to meet at my Mom's or a restaurant; someplace where I felt more comfortable. Here I was, on the steps of some stranger's home, alone, and my family didn't even know my whereabouts. I paused a moment, and then rang the doorbell.

The door swung open immediately. I came face to face with an younger version of my biological mother. I gasped, and almost bolted back to my car, but resisted the urge and stood there, speechless. Sarah had grey hair, hanging loosely in a messy bob that reached her shoulders, with the same hazel eyes as Stephanie. Her face had fewer wrinkles than I remembered Stephanie's. I supposed it was because my birth mother had abused alcohol and nicotine for many years. Sarah smiled ever so slightly and held the door open. "You must be Casandra. Come in. I've been expecting you." Then she stepped aside, still holding the door. I nodded but said nothing. It was all I could do to walk across the threshold. What had I agreed to here? Anxiety welled up in my throat; I still couldn't say anything. Sarah led the way and motioned for me to sit on her blue velour sofa. "Could I get you some lemonade? I just made it this morning."

The drive up to Springville and then on to Kent was long enough for me to replay the phone conversation with Sarah over and over in my mind. I resented the intrusion—of having to fit this trip to see her into my schedule. Plus, how did I really feel about the news of my birth mother passing? It was hard to feel sadness or remorse; only the empty feeling of abandonment—and, if I was honest, anger. Why hadn't Stephanie tried to make things right with me before it was too late? The fact that she didn't, always led back to the conclusion that she didn't care—didn't want me. Again. I had tried to connect with her, hadn't I? I had researched where she was located, discovered that she lived in Montana, and then visited her two times; more if you count the fact that I even tried living with her for a few weeks when I was eighteen.

My thoughts came back to the present. Sarah had just asked me something—if I wanted lemonade, I think. "Uh, thank you, yes," I managed to utter. I sat stiffly on the flabby sofa and glanced around the living room while she left for the kitchen. There was a fireplace, but no fire since it was still late summer. Over the mantel were pictures of happy children, two girls and a boy. A rocking chair sat opposite the sofa, but there was little else except a coffee table and one end table supporting a lamp in the sparsely furnished room. Just then Sarah reappeared, holding two large plastic glasses filled with lemonade.

"Here we go," she said cheerily, setting the glasses down on coasters already placed on the scratched coffee table. She plopped heavily into the rocking chair and looked at me, seeming to appraise me for the first time. "You look nothing like your mother." It was a statement, full of meaning, whether intended or not.

"I know—I'm much darker, right?" I wanted to bite back the question, but it was too late.

"Uh, yes, true. But there's more than that." She continued to study my face, not seeming to notice that it made me look the other way, into the kitchen. I felt so self-conscious and uncomfortable. As I did, a calico cat sauntered over and sniffed my pantlegs. It seemed satisfied and jumped up to sit beside me on the sofa. "Cindy likes you," Sarah commented. The cat was the ice breaker I desperately needed.

"Cats always like me. And I like them a lot."

"Your mother had no patience with animals in general, and cats in particular." Sarah took a sip of lemonade, setting the glass back down with emphasis.

"Or children, am I right?" I interjected with sarcasm. The question slipped out before I realized it.

"Well, about that." Sarah cleared her throat, trying to decide where to begin. She seemed at a loss and waited for me to say more. I picked up my glass and drank a couple of swallows of the liquid. It was too sour and not cold enough; I tried not to grimace as I set it back down. Silence. The cat purred, looking up at me gratefully as I stroked her lush fur from head to tail. Since I didn't say anything more, she plunged into the topic of Stephanie. "So, like I mentioned over the phone, Stephanie had a will, even though her material possessions were very few. She wanted to make certain that when she passed, you would be contacted." She paused and gave me a look that asked me to encourage her to proceed.

"Okay," I said, just to keep the topic moving.

"So, let me get the will and the letter. Just a moment." She got up out of the rocker, which kept rocking long after she disappeared in the direction of the bedroom hallway. I sat, still petting the Cindy cat, glad that I had her for a diversion. Why would a mother who gave up her only child—at least I assumed I was the only child—mention her in a will? Perplexing.

Sarah returned within moments, carrying a manila folder. She withdrew a sheet of paper, and sat back down, this time next to Cindy on the sofa. "Here's the will. You may read it, but first I will read the main part: 'I hereby wish to give all my possessions or items of any worth solely to my beloved daughter, Casandra McMillen of Springville, Washington.' This was dated and signed in 1986—two years after you were born, right?"

"Uh, yes, that's right." The word "beloved" stuck in my mind and swirled around in the anger and disappointment I had always felt toward Stephanie.

"Do you want to read the rest of it now or later?"

"Later." It was all I could do to keep my indignation under control. I wanted to scoff—to turn around and stomp out the door. Sarah must have picked up on my feelings, putting the will back into the folder.

"So, here is the letter. I think it best for you to read it for yourself," she added gently. At that, she pulled out another paper, a handwritten one, the scrawl of it unfamiliar to me. "Stephanie wrote this, and it is dated May of 2001." Sarah handed it over to me. I didn't want to pick it up; my hand trembled; but I lifted it gently and began to read.

May 2, 2001

My dearest daughter, Casandra,
I am writing this to you, but you may not see this until I have departed out of this world. My life was a constant stream of failures, one after another, until I met your father, Robert Harris. Because of him, I became a mother and bore you. You are the one thing I did in this life that I am proud

of. Because of you, my life had meaning. I loved you from the instant you were conceived, which I knew in my heart from the earliest moment, when you were probably just a tiny glimmer in your father's eye.

At that point in the letter, my heart lurched; I even had trouble breathing. I stopped for a moment, and raised my eyes to look over at Sarah, who nodded encouragingly for me to continue. My hands shook; the paper quivered—but I read on.

There wasn't a day that I didn't talk to you while you were in my womb. I shared my joys and heartaches with you, which were mostly heartaches. But you were my joy. I yearned to see you, and patiently counted down the nine months, hoping against hope that you would love me in return, and be a healthy baby.

Your father was a good man, but he had high aspirations for his future. You and I clouded that future. When I shared the news of my pregnancy with him, he disappeared. I never saw him again. I had hoped that you would bring us together permanently, as a family. Perhaps we would even marry, your father and me. It wasn't meant to be, because he left. As the pregnancy continued, which of course, I wished it to continue, I became very obviously pregnant. The job became too difficult in my condition, and I could no longer work there. After about seven months, I had to leave my job as a waitress. I was living month to month, you see, and barely got by while I was working. The last months of pregnancy were extremely difficult financially. My family had forbidden me to return home, so I was totally alone, afraid, and nearly thrown out on the street. I got by until you were born by taking in laundry and ironing for a dry cleaner nearby. It wasn't enough to live on, but I managed to pay the rent with it. I applied for food stamps to survive.

When you were born, I couldn't believe my joy. You were the perfect little baby girl, with enormous brown eyes, and black hair. You were so unlike me, with bleached, mousey brown hair, hazel eyes, and pale-white skin. You were so beautiful as I gazed at you in wonder, your complexion, a creamy caramel. You were so fragile, petite, and perfect. What was I to do? I couldn't provide for myself, let alone a child. I would have to find another waitress job because that's all I had experience in. I was barely nineteen when you were born and had no training in anything else. There would be no money for childcare, and even if there were, how could I leave such a beautifully perfect baby all day?

I wanted you to have the opportunities I never had. To get an education, to have two parents who loved you, to have a family, everything! I cried all day, the day after you were born. I didn't know what to do. Finally, the nurse at the hospital asked me why I was crying, and I told her my dilemma. That's when the doctor came in and told me he knew of an agency who was looking for a baby for a lovely couple. I wept at that, trying to come to the decision to give you up. I loved you so very much, Casandra. But because I put you first, I gave you to the nice couple.

I hope your life has been good so far. Mine only has meaning if your life is good. I will always love you. Please don't judge me too harshly.

      Stephane Hoffman, your mother

Before I had finished reading the last sentence of the letter, the page was already full of droplets from my tears. Would Stephanie have approved of how my life was turning out so far? Had I already let down her expectations for me? I couldn't look up yet; my eyes were blurry and moist, and I felt self-conscious. I kept my head down by rereading the letter, which only further heightened the emotional tears. At last, I handed back the letter to Sarah, but said nothing. She took it from me and lovingly placed the letter back into the envelope.

"So, Casandra, that is your mother's story. From her own hand." Sarah spoke softly, unsure of what to say next. The Cindy cat purred as I stroked her velvety, black, brown, and white fur, relieved to have the cat as a diversion. I still said nothing, trying to process what I had just read. "There was one more thing that was included with the letter and will," she said, reaching back into the manila envelope. She withdrew a small parcel, wrapped in tissue paper. I took it from her extended hand and unwrapped the paper. Inside was a locket on a chain. "The few times I saw Stephanie after your birth, she was always wearing the locket. It was on a long chain which dangled close to her heart. But she never allowed me to see inside. It's yours now."

Opening the locket, I found a tiny picture of a newborn baby, just the face. The baby had black hair and a mocha face. It was me.

"Oh! I didn't know," was all I managed to say.

Chapter 13

On the way to Tully's condo in Springville, I reviewed my visit to Sarah. Before I had left Sarah's, she introduced me to her son, saying, "Kevin, meet your cousin, Casandra." I nearly withdrew my hand in shock and revulsion.

"Uh, did you say cousin?" And by the way, people call me Cassie." Grudgingly, I took Kevin's hand, who stood there waiting to shake mine.

"Hi, Cuz. Glad to finally meet you," he said, beaming at me, shaking my hand longer than necessary. Kevin was dressed in baggy sweatpants and a tee shirt. He looked to be a few years younger than I, with long, brown hair, and the same hazel eyes as Sarah. And Stephanie's—I could see it.

"So, I see that you met my mom. She would be your aunt, right?" He glanced playfully over to her, and then back to me.

"Wow, isn't that a revelation? Who knew?" I retorted with sarcasm, trying to recover from the news. I started to realize that here were relatives I never knew existed, just a few miles from where I grew up, and I find out only after my natural mother's demise.

Why didn't she tell me that she had a sister with children? And living near Springville even? What the heck? I felt betrayed—left out of the loop for my entire life. The old resentment and anger welled up in my stomach. I kept driving but needed to stop for a soda to calm my nerves. I pulled over into a gas station and lurched inside to the convenience store. I grabbed a lemon lime soda, paid, and unscrewed the cap for a swallow. It fizzed and burned all the way down. No relief—only more acid to my nervous stomach. I couldn't face Mom just yet, so next, I pulled off at a strip mall, and browsed around aimlessly through a couple of clothing stores. Styles had changed since I had shopped last, and prices were higher than I remembered because I shopped as seldom as possible. I tried on some jeans and ended up buying a pair. The purchasing activity at least calmed me down a bit before moving on to Mom's.

As I ascended the stairs to Mom's condo, the fragrant aroma of spaghetti wafted down. I smiled to myself, realizing that she was preparing it because I was arriving; spaghetti was my favorite meal. I let myself in and meandered into the kitchen. It was as I had dreaded. Both Mom and Jasmine awaited, ready to pommel me with questions. I glimpsed Jasmine's strawberry blonde hair from the doorway, bent over the counter. "Hi, Mom. Hey, Jasmine." I gave Mom a half hug. Jasmine nodded, kept chopping, and only looked up once.

Mom smiled over the steamy pot of sauce, returning the hug, and added a peck on the cheek. "Welcome home, Cassie."

"Hi Cass," Jasmine finally greeted me. "So, you drove up here to Washington, but not to see us. To follow up on your natural dad search, right? Please—give me a break. Why are you so obsessed with finding this mystery father of yours? We just lost Dad a few years ago. Have some respect." Jasmine knew I had gone to Sarah's in Kent, which was the reason for my visit to Springville.

"Can you at least let me get in the door before giving me the third degree? Thanks for the welcome greeting, Sis." Jasmine just glared at me, and then looked down, continuing her salad making.

"Maybe that's the point," Mom returned, facing Jasmine. "You and Cassie lost your Dad. Grief brings things out." I looked over to Mom appreciatively. She seemed to understand, at least partially, and gave me a second hug. Then she returned to the stove to stir the pot, and Jasmine continued cutting vegetables for a salad, suddenly focusing intently on precise chopping.

"It smells delicious! Thanks for cooking spaghetti, Mom."

"Of course. You haven't been home in a while. Happy to see you and cook something you like." Mom grinned over the fragrant sauce, adding some basil. I sat down on a chair and watched my two adopted family members at work. It was odd; now I knew that I had blood relatives nearby. But Mom and Jasmine asked me nothing; it was as if I had merely gone out to the store and back, not just met my real family and read my dead mother's will and letter. It hit me with such force; I couldn't share anything with these two. At least, not today. Maybe someday, after I had time to process it a little more.

When I returned home to my apartment in Corvallis, I hauled in the boxes of things of Stephanie's that were willed to me and handed over to me by Sarah. My Aunt Sarah. What a new concept! I never knew I had an Aunt Sarah until she telephoned me about Stephanie's death. There wasn't much of value in the boxes, just a few knick-knacks and books. Then, in the very bottom of the box, I uncovered a picture album. As I turned the pages of the album, there he was: my father, Robert Harris. Stephanie had owned a picture of him all along, and never shared it with me. She had labeled the picture, "Bobby." There was one more photo of the two of them together, looking into one another's eyes, so visibly in love. I felt cheated once more: why didn't she let me see these? Thumbing through more pages, I came upon photos of me, a newborn. My breath caught as I saw the tender expression on Stephanie's face as she held me, wrapped in a fuzzy pink blanket. A tiny, dark face peeked out from under a pink cap. Stephanie had written a caption underneath which said, "My sweet baby girl, Casandra."

"Oh!" I uttered out loud. Tears moistened the aging photos as I wept uncontrollably. Just seeing the pictures gave me an insight into Stephanie, a part of her that she had never allowed me to fathom. It was clear that she loved the infant, namely me, whom she had given birth to. But how on earth did she decide to just throw me away? Why??? Better yet, why did my father disappear after learning of her pregnancy? How could he do that? How could either of them do this to me, an innocent child? To think that we could have been a real family. The loss hit me full force; I cried anew. After a few more minutes, I replaced the album in the box and closed the lid, vowing to never look at it again. It hurt too much.

Chapter 14
Fall 2008

This time the shuttle dropped me off at a mid-price hotel on South Padre Island instead of the cheap youth hostel. I felt like I had grown up enough to get a proper hotel and besides, Claire would share the cost of the room with me. She told me that Preston intended to reserve at the same hotel as well. It was October, with affordable off-season rates. As the bus pulled up, I saw palm trees waving in the breeze to greet me. It was good to be back in a tropical setting, even though my stomach was already turning flip flops remembering the horrific occurrence on the beach that fateful night with the jerk, Ramon. I fervently hoped that I wouldn't run into him while I was here on the island. It was a small place—especially off season. Tourists were noticeably fewer now.

I grabbed my bag, stood straight, and marched in. I had to try this once more. I arranged to meet Dr. Jordan's friend, Guy Collins, to attempt to figure out where my real father was. I stepped up to the check-in counter and gave my name, Casandra McMillen. As the clerk searched for my room number, I heard a shriek. "You're here, girlfriend!" Claire stood before me, her red hair glistening on end in its spikey do. She pulled me into a hug before I could catch a breath. "She's with me," Claire said to the clerk. "I already got your key to the room, so you don't need to check in."

When she released me from the tight hug, I finally caught my breath. "Great! Good to see you, Claire! I missed you." I smiled wanly, hoping she didn't sense my anxiety of being on the island after the assault. She seemed oblivious; just snatched my bag and commanded me to follow her to our room on the third floor. We took an elevator up and soon I found myself looking out onto a view of the Laguna Madre Bay.

"I had forgotten how beautiful and peaceful this place is," I murmured, gazing out the open window. I could feel the island air wafting in gently. I turned to see that Claire was bent over her suitcase, sorting out clothes.

"I'm checking to see what I want to put on for tonight," she said, holding up a red blouse, and inspecting it before tossing it onto the bed.

"Why, what's tonight?" I asked mildly, not thinking that far ahead. I had only just arrived, after all.

"Well, we are meeting Preston and another guy over dinner down at the club. You know the one. It has dancing and live music."

"Oh, yeah, the Carmela Club. I remember. We started to go last time, but I left for home early. Never went." The traumatic scene came up in my mind at the mention of leaving early. My heart skipped a little with trepidation. I hesitated, and Claire seemed to pick up on my fear.

"It's going to be okay, Cassie. Don't worry. Preston and I won't let you out of our sight. We'll do everything as a group this time, except maybe when you meet with the butterfly person. You'll be safe with us as well as with the old insect man."

"Right. His name is Guy Collins, and I don't know his age. But I suppose he is an older man, since he knows my father and also Dr. Jordan." I took a deep breath, then continued. "I'll be fine. Just a few jitters. It hasn't been all that long ago that I was here, and I met this, this, …"

"Ass hole," Claire finished.

"Right. Ass hole for sure. But I'm trying to face my fears to come back here to get the information I need to find my father. Hopefully, Guy Collins will have some needed info for me."

"You are brave and strong. You can do it." Claire took my hand and then gave me a hug. I realized then that with my friends beside me, I could do it. I had returned to the scene of the devastating event—the date rape— and knew I could accomplish what I had set out to do the first time I visited the island. I was so fortunate to have supportive friends willing to meet me her.

"We're not having a 'date' or anything, tonight, are we? I'm not up for that just yet." The pit in my stomach seized up at the thought.

"No. no, of course not. Just meeting up as friends with Preston and his friend. That's all." Claire smiled a little too brightly, and I could see behind it. I decided to ignore it and go with it. After all, she claimed that she and Preston would protect me. I was too tired to protest after the long flight from Oregon. I had left Corvallis at two o'clock that morning, drove up to Portland and caught my flight. It was already dinner time here in Texas. Reluctantly, I opened my suitcase to see what I would wear tonight. I pulled out a black top with flowy sleeves, and a new pair of skinny jeans. The outfit would have to do.

THE BAND WAS SO LOUD THAT I MISSED HEARING THE NAME OF Preston's friend. Later, I heard Preston call his friend Tommy. Tommy Cho was also from San Francisco, where Preston lived. They had been friends since middle school. He too, had cropped jet black hair and narrow black eyes. He was tall, trim and almost willowy in his slimness, whereas Preston was solid, stocky, and broad chested. Tommy seemed shy; he just kept smiling as Preston and Claire chattered away with the music blasting. I couldn't make out a word they were saying, so Tommy probably couldn't either. We all sat on stools at a small table with our margaritas. I was super cautious; I never lost sight of my open drink, preferring to sip on it without letting go of the glass until it was finished. There would be no risk of it being tampered with an ecstasy elixir from anyone in the establishment. Claire glanced at it only once, understanding in her eyes. She knew what I was doing but said nothing. Only after I had downed it completely did she suggest going to the ladies' room. "No worries. Both Preston and Tommy are harmless. Just friends. Am I right?" She arched her brows and pushed the restroom door open.

"Well, right. I'm just not taking any chances on anyone in the bar messing with my drink this time. You never know."

When we returned to our seats, the band was on break. Finally. I could hear what was being discussed. Preston and Tommy had just reordered drinks for themselves, and Preston asked, "You ladies want anything more to drink?" We both declined. I was already feeling heady. "We were discussing what to do tomorrow as a group. How about we do that dolphin cruise thing? Sounds fun to see dolphins from the boat. Are you both in?" He looked over at Claire and me expectantly. It did sound fun. I guess I could wait another day before trying to meet up with Guy Collins. I had seven days here—there was still plenty of time.

"Sure, let's do it!" Claire turned to me for my answer. I nodded yes, so we agreed to meet after breakfast at eleven or so and venture out to the marina. It sounded like an enjoyable—and safe—activity for the day. Ahead of the cruise, we planned to picnic at the island's farthest point, the South Padre Island Park. When Preston and Tommy volunteered to bring the lunch, Claire and I readily agreed. They both wore cargo shorts and tees for the outing since it was sunny and warm. Claire and I decided on cutoff jeans, so we all were dressed for the sun and recreation, even though it was late October. They carried lunch in a backpack, complete with a small tablecloth to cover a picnic table. The guys brought delicious deli ham and Swiss on rye sandwiches, chips, and canned sodas. After they put out the lunch, we ate greedily, since breakfast was only a bagel and coffee. Birds circled overhead as we heard the lull of soothing waves lapping the shore. I watched as a flock of small sandpipers dodged the waves. Tommy finally loosened up a bit and talked a little. "We bought this at Terry's Deli near the hotel," he stated, trying to get a conversation of his own going.

"Excellent choice. These sandwiches are delicious," Claire answered, with mayonnaise dripping out of her lips as she spoke. She grabbed her napkin and wiped her mouth, giggling. I nodded agreement since my mouth was too full to say anything. We ate every bite, including chips and an apple for each of us. For dessert, they pulled out thick slices of cheesecake, which went down smooth and rich. Regretfully, it was time to leave the stunning views in the park, and we slowly meandered our way to the nearby marina to catch our boat ride.

THE DOLPHIN BOAT, A CATAMARAN, WAS EQUIPPED TO CARRY twenty-five or so people. The boat appeared to be at capacity, and we had to split up to find a place to sit. Once we were at sea, however, we were permitted to walk around, searching the water for dolphins. The skipper acted as tour guide, pointing out the sights as well as the dolphins. Our phone cameras were in constant use, trying to capture the swift movements of dolphins as they cavorted alongside the boat. Occasionally, a dolphin came so close, the skipper commented that the animal was trying to catch a peek at us. All the dolphins seemed to enjoy themselves, opening their mouths wide in joy, leaping into the air and then diving down into the depths of the water. We all exclaimed together with "Ahs!" and "Ohs!" as the dolphins performed their acrobatic feats. Overhead, we saw pelicans flying in solemn formation, then suddenly pointing themselves into nosedives to retrieve fish. We had chosen a sunset cruise and admired the shoreline and island bridge which served as backdrop for the setting sun— a spectacular sight!

"I love this!" I shouted out once. Everyone on board murmured their agreement. It truly was delightful. The skipper seemed to know exactly where to turn the boat to capture the ultimate number of dolphins as well as the stunning sunset view.

Our two-hour excursion ended all too soon; it became dark quickly in the October sky; the boat returned slowly to the marina to dock. As we disembarked, Claire nearly tripped. "My sea legs aren't working right." Everyone on board chuckled. I nearly stumbled as well.

"Shall we debrief at Beach Bums?" Preston suggested. I swallowed hard—that was the place where I had left with that monster a year ago. I dreaded going back.

"Sure, why not?" Claire answered, staring straight at me. I knew I had to face my fears, so I nodded slowly. I would get that part over with.

"What's at Beach Bums?" Tommy asked innocently.

"Cheap burgers and beers," Preston retorted.

That isn't all, I thought nervously. Hopefully, Ramon wouldn't be there.

Chapter 15

"I embrace emerging experience. I participate in discovery. I am not a butterfly collector. I want the experience of the butterfly."

—William Stafford

Our time at Beach Bums was uneventful, except for eating their typical burgers washed down with beer. I peered around in the dimly lit pub, but there was, thankfully, no sign of Ramon. I breathed a little easier but remained on high alert as Claire, Preston, and Tommy chatted and recapped our dolphin excursion. The burger I ate went down greasy, the beer, bitter. Everything formed a ball in my stomach which then turned into a big knot. Soon, I felt stifled; I couldn't breathe. Still, they all droned on happily about the sightings of the dolphins, the sunset, the pelicans, and the other passengers on board the catamaran. I felt as though I would be sick and excused myself to the ladies' room—but only after finishing my drink. I still didn't take any chances that someone might drop something in my drink—especially in this God-forsaken pub. The terror of last years' experience loomed in the front of my mind by being there again. I threw up in the toilet, calmly wiped my mouth, and rinsed at the sink. When I returned from the restroom, I ordered a club soda with lime. Claire kept glancing over at me, questioningly, to make sure I was doing okay. I just looked down into my glass, stirred the ice, and tried not to make eye contact. I managed to get through the evening, and we all returned to the hotel around nine. It was only in the hotel room that I allowed myself to relax.

"I wasn't sure you were going to make it at Beach Bums. But you did it, Cassie."

"Yeah, I did. But it was hard. I relived that night all over again. Plus, I got sick in the bathroom."

"Oh, sorry, girlfriend. I was afraid of that. But it will get easier with time. Trust me. Just remember, Preston and I are here for you."

"Does he know?" My heart lurched at the thought. I was already getting into my pajamas and hoping to forget Beach Bums for the night.

"Oh, no. Nothing like that," Claire said a little too quickly. "But we are all here together. I told him you just need time with us as friends, and you have to find your father through the butterfly man."

I was restless in the night, my mind going from the dolphins leaping in midair, to the rape on the beach near Beach Bums a year ago. Finally, I dreamed of meeting my father, who, in my fitful dream, hugged me and spoke to me of his desire to connect with me as his daughter. When I awoke, I was starving. I had lost my dinner last night and my empty stomach rumbled in protest. I ate an early breakfast, complimentary amenity of the hotel. Later that day, the four of us visited the sea turtle rescue and hospital. I was glad for the distraction and enjoyed learning how people were dedicated to saving the sea turtle population.

The following day, on Wednesday, I finally was able to contact Dr. Jordan's friend, Guy Collins by phone. We agreed to meet on Thursday at the island birding center at eleven thirty. He gave directions, and the next day, I took the island bus to get there. I wasn't sure what Guy looked like, only that he must be an older gentleman. I assured Claire I would be fine to go alone. I stepped off the bus and checked my surroundings. It was a long walk through a parking lot, before I reached the entrance to the birding center building. Outside the door stood an older man, obviously waiting for someone. I approached, inquiring cautiously, "Are you Guy Collins by any chance?"

"That's the name," he said, reaching out to shake my hand. "And you must be Casandra McMillen." His smile softly embraced me. I liked him immediately.

AT LONG LAST I WAS HERE: IN THE BUTTERFLY GARDEN OF THE birding center on South Padre Island. Monarch butterflies were grouped in a dazzling array, glistening in the sunlight. They had migrated from points north, and rested there in the foliage, clumped in large orange and black groups, like many flower blossoms. The spectacle took my breath away. Guy stood back, smiling, as I kept exclaiming over and over at the astounding array in front of me. "Are they like this every October?" I asked, turning to look back at him. He had his telephoto lens out, clicking away, and nodded.

"Yes, but sometimes they wait until November. However, usually they come in late October." I walked slowly, from one tree or flowering bush to another, overwhelmed at the resplendence. The butterfly garden was named for the purposefully planted flowers that the overwintering, or migrating butterflies were attracted to. They needed the nutrients that these particular flowers afforded, and which bloomed in accordance with the season of migration. There was yellow goldenrod, the lovely red Turk's cap, and a blue type of flower that he didn't identify. I was too distracted to catch all the details. We said little, just beholding the gorgeous clustering of the black and orange butterflies reposing on branches and petals. They dwarfed the artistry of the flower blossoms, so magnificent as their wings gently opened and shut, reflecting sunrays, or just remained closed. Guy pointed out other species of butterflies as well. We observed an occasional bluish-black butterfly and many pale-yellow sulfur butterflies, a striking contrast to the bold orange and black Monarchs.

"Come, let me show you the view from the top of the building.". I followed Guy silently, as we wound our way out of the garden and into the building. At the top, on the fifth-level tower, we looked out at the expanse. One could see the vista of the narrow island, from the Gulf, all the way to the Madre Laguna. Pelicans flew overhead in groups as sentinels, scanning the water below them. I heard the rush of wind and occasionally the waves, in the distance.

"It's magnificent up here!" I turned to Guy, and he grinned again, his eyes crinkling at the corners. I noticed his silver, receding hair tucked under his brimmed cap to protect his weathered face from the sun. He was slight in build but stood upright. He mentioned that he had retired ten years ago, but still loved to volunteer at the center as a tour guide for people interested in the butterflies.

"I am not exactly a lepidopterist, because I have never enjoyed pinning a dead butterfly's wings. I just observe and study them in the wild, and photograph their amazing elegance," Guy explained. I watched as he pointed out different points of the island, detailing how the island had built up in construction over the years. Back on ground level, we toured around the long boardwalk of the birding center, observing the different types of exotic and dazzling birds. He drew attention to the white Great Egret and Snowy Egret, the Roseate Spoonbill, pink from their diet of shrimp, and Common

Gallinules, which he compared to chickens. We observed many species of ducks as well as the Tropical Kingbird, Red-winged Blackbird, and others. My favorite was the Great Blue Heron, which Guy said had a wingspan of six feet.

The boardwalk jutted out into the Madre Laguna, a salty body of water which emptied out into the Gulf of Mexico, and then the walkway curved around into fresh water as well. Different species of wildlife inhabited each area. Alligators, which we also observed, thrived in the freshwater. We circled back through the butterfly garden once more before leaving, to imprint the striking allure to memory.

"So, there we are, Casandra. These are the Monarchs. If you wish, we could go for coffee down the street and talk. Would you like that?" Guy offered.

"Yes, oh yes! Let's talk. I need to ask about someone you know. My—my father." For some reason, just saying that made me feel embarrassed. What would he think of me now? Would he think me foolish for attempting to track down my father after all this time?

Guy's expression remained emotionless when I mentioned my father. For a nano second, I thought that perhaps it was a purposeful, inscrutable blankness. He just replied, "Of course. I have my car here, so let's hop in and drive to the coffee shop."

Chapter 16

"Do you know my father, Robert Harris?"

Guy Collins smiled before answering; his right hand cupped around his coffee mug as we sat in a booth in the back of the coffee shop. I waited anxiously. I had come to this island on two separate occasions for the sole purpose of asking Guy Collins about my father's whereabouts. It was such a long shot, and now that I was sitting across from this man, it scared me. What if he had no information at all? My search would dead end here on this tiny island off the Texas shore. Guy paused, seeming to drag out the tension for me on purpose. He took a sip off his coffee and set the cup down. What was he about to answer? I dreaded it—yet longed for him to say something—anything.

The elderly man shifted in his seat a moment, as if attempting to sort out how to answer. "So, Casandra, what have you discovered so far about your father?" He searched my face, and our eyes met for a second.

"Well, all I know is that as a young man he studied at Oregon State, in Corvallis, in the biology department. He was interested in the migration of the Monarch Butterfly and hoping to learn more to counteract their population decline. Of course, I also know that he met my biological mother, Stephanie Hoffman, and that she became pregnant from their relationship." I tittered nervously after making such a rhetorical comment. I continued after taking a swallow of my coffee. "I met Dr. Jordan after asking around at the university, and found out from him that indeed, Robert Harris was an intern there in the biology department, to study the migration. Then Dr. Jordan told me to contact you, personally, on the island. So here I am." I again waited, hoping for the information I was so desperately searching for.

"Okay." He drew a deep breath before proceeding. "Well, your father, Robert Harris, or Bob, was a student of mine at the university. He interned under my direction, in fact. After he graduated, he came out to this island to observe the migration of the Monarchs. I think he stayed for two seasons, maybe three. I met up with him here twice during the annual fall migration. That was way before there was a tourist place, like a birding center. We just hung out and hiked around the island, photographing what we could, making field notes and whatever we could do to document what we observed. Bob took up residency here for those two or three years. I had to get back to Corvallis for teaching, you know, but he was young and ambitious. He wanted to change the world with his findings." At that, Guy chuckled a little, seeming to remember things about my father that he would not reveal to me—at least, not now.

"So, what happened? Where is he now?" I thought I would run out of patience waiting for real information of his whereabouts. I toyed with my napkin and waited. My coffee was too cold to drink now. I pushed the cup away from me. Why is he hesitating?

"Casandra, your father was a driven man. He pursued his dream of helping the Monarchs at all costs." Guy stopped, saying nothing.

"So, what does that mean? What happened to him?" I felt panic rise in my throat; I couldn't swallow, and my stomach clenched. Was he about to tell me I had reached the end of my search? What happened to my father?

"Let's see. I think I last saw him here on the island during the fall migration of about 1986, I believe. We worked together for a month or so, during late October and early November. I had taken some time off fall term at the university to do some research here. Hmmm." Guy seemed to search the ceiling for more to say. I moved to the edge of my seat in the booth. I could barely contain myself and held my breath. "So, I heard back from him by telephone around January or so. That would have been early in 1987. Bob had applied for another grant to study the Monarch migration habits in Mexico from a university in Monterey. He mentioned wanting to track the Monarchs to their final migration destination in Mexico. That was the last I heard of him. I assume he went there next. The Monarchs usually arrive down there in February to March."

"Wh-what was the name of the university there?" I felt desperation hover at the edges of my mind, realizing now that I was venturing into a totally futile search.

"Let me see," Guy paused, again looking up to search his memory. "It was a name in Spanish….in Monterey, Mexico, like I mentioned. Hmm, something like, oh yes: Universidad Autonoma de Nuevo Leon?"

"What was that again?" I retrieved my small notebook and a pen from my purse to jot the name down. I nervously wrote, hoping I spelled everything correctly. Fortunately, I had bothered to take two years of Spanish in high school, so I understood the basics.

He repeated the name of the university again and looked over my notes to see if I got it right. "Yes. Correct. The state is Leon in Mexico. City is Monterey. It's really not that far from the island. Just across the border a way. If you obtain your passport, I'm sure you will have no trouble finding it. I think Bob was accepted in their biology department. They have quite a large campus, I'm told." Guy was attempting to cheer me up. I must have looked the way I felt deflated—discouraged. Nothing he said now would help.

The server came by and refilled our coffee cups. I sighed, taking a sip off the fresh coffee. I had made the trip to the island two times, only to find out that this friend of my father's had not seen or heard from him since 1987, and that my father had traipsed off to a university in Mexico. He could be anywhere by now—or worse, dead. It was a long time ago and I was still so far from my goal: to find my father.

Chapter 17

Back in the hotel room, I flung myself on the bed, and sobbed uncontrollably. I just couldn't face the thought of this being the end of my quest to find my father. I had invested so much effort and time already. But what was the use? The one person who might know of his whereabouts hadn't seen or heard from him since I was three years old. And that was before my father headed out to Mexico. How would I ever find him there? It was a huge and sometimes terrifying country, what with cartels, corruption, and the dangers to a young American woman alone. The enormity and hopelessness of my search came down full force. What was I thinking?

As I lay there feeling sorry for myself, Claire unlocked the door and walked in, interrupting my reverie. "Hey, girlfriend, what's going on? How was your meeting with the butterfly man?" She threw her purse on the other bed and sat down on mine.

I looked up, my eyes a swollen red mess. "It's hopeless, Claire. This was all a stupid pipe dream to find my dad."

"Oh, sorry girl. Did you find out that he's dead or what?" Claire bent down, rubbing my back, trying to soothe my tears.

"I don't know. Worse, actually. He went to Mexico in 1987 and hasn't been heard of since. I'll never find him now. I'll never figure my life out. He was the key." I sniffed, reaching for a tissue on the nightstand. "And for sure I can't go wandering around Mexico by myself. It's not smart or safe."

"Well, who says we can't all go to Mexico and look for him?" Claire grabbed my hands in hers, forcing me to sit up. "Our new adventure—a new destination!" She smiled encouragingly, making me laugh in spite of myself. "

"Really? You would do that? I knew we were friends, but this? Do you think we could all go—and Preston too, as our bodyguard?" I hadn't thought of any of this before. These were such good and dear friends, but to drag them around Mexico? I wasn't sure.

"Absolutely. This is too important for you to drop the search now. Plus, it could be fun! People go to Mexico to vacation, you know. We'll ask Preston tonight over dinner. Maybe even ask Tommy? I don't know about him. We've only just met him. Tonight, we plan to eat next door at the little Chinese place. Sounds good, right?" Claire was definitely trying to get me to quit crying and think of something else.

"Uh, okay. I guess. Let's go for early dinner. I don't feel like staying out late tonight."

"Sure. I'll call Preston and ask him to be ready at five and we'll head over to eat and talk about our next adventure!" Claire sounded so positive and enthusiastic; it was hard to keep crying. I dried my face and got ready.

"SINCE IT'S ALREADY LATE OCTOBER, WE WILL HAVE TO HURRY to apply for passports in time to go for the winter migration in Mexico," I said in between bites of chow Mein. It was interesting to watch Preston and Tommy at work on their Chinese food, expertly using chopsticks. I fumbled around with the sticks and finally gave in to shoveling my food with a fork. I noticed that Claire was doing the same. "I read that the best time to observe the Monarchs in Mexico is from late January to the end of March. Maybe we could try for late February or early March. My best chance to find my father is probably during the winter migration— if he's even there at all." I sighed, considering how difficult this search was becoming. "Plus, I have to ask for more time off, and you probably do, too, right Claire?"

"Well, sure. But my job is fairly flexible, since I work for an ad agency. I can do some stuff ahead of time, and just say I'll be gone a week or so." She looked at me reassuringly, seeming to know just what to say to build up my enthusiasm.

"So, why not bypass the university, since it's been so long ago that your father went there, and go straight to the area of the winter migration?" Preston piped up at last, and Tommy nodded his approval of the idea.

"Are you saying you'll go too?" My heart skipped, thinking that this hopeless search might not be so insurmountable after all.

"Why not? I'm all about new adventures. I live with my folks, so right now I'm not working. Plus, going there may help me in my novel writing. Maybe my 'great Chinese- American novel' character can take an interest in Monarch migration." He chuckled at his own joke.

Tommy giggled a little, and finally implored, "Do you think I could come too?" His face appeared nearly childlike, as if we would turn him down. "I'm sure I can get time off from my job at the restaurant. People are always looking for more hours."

"Sure. The more the merrier, right Cassie?" Claire took a bite of eggroll, glancing my way for an answer.

"Let's see if we can all get passports in time and also be able to take time off," I answered, thinking of the hurdles ahead of us for such a trip.

"How about we start this by seeing the migrating butterflies right here on the island? We could go tomorrow morning. We still have a couple of days left here." Preston grinned, and excitement twinkled in his black eyes. His positive energy was hard to resist.

Winter Moon

The sky is pitch black, with cheerless, gloomy clouds.

The moon peers out, frigid and bleak,
a three-quarter portion

of frozen planet.

The other slice remains obscured, as if ashamed.

The polar air pierces, nipping through layers
of wool, fleece, and flannel

As people hunch and shiver, stepping gingerly
over ice laden sidewalks.

A mottled brown feral cat slithers out from a bush,
longing for shelter and food only rarely found.

The crescent casts a pale light onto the barren,
whispering, branches.

There will be no respite until spring.
No promise of life, only arctic, frosty expectation.
Endurance is expedient.

The homeless feline slinks on, unwilling to give in
to a cold death. Her face is ghostly with despair,
but she keeps moving, a fragment of yearning to
chance upon sustenance for the day.

There will be no place to thaw her frozen paws.

PART 2
Mexico

Chapter 18

As it turned out, it was too difficult to get us all together for a trip to Mexico in only a few months' time. We all needed to work and save up again. We decided to plan on it for the following year and go late February or early March of 2010. I fretted over the delay. Each month was one more postponement of finding out who I was through discovering my real father. I just knew that I had to find him; it became an obsession.

Then, at the last minute, I received a phone call for an interview as a news correspondent journalist. I thought nothing of it—after all, I had been applying for over a year at that point, with no success. The position was with the local news station, but they needed a roving news journalist. I called for an interview, which was set for the next day. I met with the feature news editor, Janice, who hired me on the spot. She asked where I might want to go for my first out of the area assignment. "Really? You're asking me to go where?" I was dumbfounded. I could name my location!

"Yes, this is a new position for us, so we are open to new ideas," Janice answered. "Do you have a place in mind?" Her large brown eyes peered over her reading glasses, and she smiled encouragingly. She looked to be a no-nonsense journalist, with brown hair tied back in a ponytail. She wore a tweed sweater and grey skirt, and tall black boots.

"As matter of fact, I do. I would like to go to Mexico next month, in February. I already applied for my passport, so it should be arriving any day. I was going to wait for next year to go but would love to go as soon as possible. I'm trying to find my father, and I think that he studies the Monarch butterfly migration down there which takes place each winter to early spring." I felt a bit foolish, hoping that she would understand the urgency of such a request. Janice had no problem with it, since I could cover the trip with a story. As we discussed possibilities, she asked if I could go to a pyramid excavation site, as well as cover the butterfly migration. How could I turn this opportunity down? It was almost too good to be true. And I would get paid for my research this time. I called Mom first to let her know of my new job as news correspondent.

"Cassie, I'm so proud of you! I knew you would land a journalist position one day. Just take care. It's not always safe in Mexico."

"I know, I know, Mom. But Claire and Preston will join up with me eventually. We'll be safe, don't worry. Let Jasmine know, too." I thought how she would react, and I didn't really want to call her at the moment. I had so much to do to get ready. She would say that I would worry Mom too much. But I had to do this. I had to pursue my dreams—to find my father as well as be a journalist.

When I called Claire and Preston about it, they were surprised and excited for me. They would try to move up their plans to join up with me after I reached the biosphere of the butterfly reserves. Of course, they would talk to Tommy to see if he could move up his plans as well. The trouble was, the biosphere, or the area where most of the Monarchs migrated to in Mexico, was a rather large geographical area, running from the eastern perimeter of the state of Michoacán, and bordering the state of Mexico in the forested mountains west of Mexico City. (A point of reference in studying a map is that the capital city of Michoacan is Morelia.) In addition, there were four designated sanctuaries within this biosphere to protect the Monarchs. Two reserves, El Rosario, near the town of Ocampo, and Sierra Chinua, near Angangueo, both in Michoacán, were the most frequented by tourists. The other two reserves were located in the state of Mexico. I researched this biosphere online to get a strategical plan for where to try to find my father. It was going to be a potentially long and arduous search, but I decided to begin with the two reserves in Michoacán. My first stop would be Angangueo, a destination reachable by tours departing out of Mexico City. For those who preferred, a person could stay over in a local hotel in Angangueo. I hoped to do that, and perhaps, eventually, Claire and Preston could join me there.

I learned that after the butterflies arrived in the area, they clung to tree trunks for most of the overwintering stay. If the sun warmed them during the day, the countless Monarchs would flutter around the forests, creating a spectacular sight for the beholder. I looked forward to this experience. But most of all, hoped to find my elusive father, Robert Harris.

By late February, I was on my way on a flight bound for Mexico City. From there, I would board a bus to ride to Puebla, a large city in the state of Puebla. From Puebla, I took a city bus to the outlying area of Cholula, the site of a partially excavated pyramid, the Pyramid of Cholula. Cholula was a quaint, picturesque town, with stucco homes and businesses, and narrow streets. As I rode the bus, I felt the other passengers staring at my Afro frizzy hair, and then quickly look away, realizing I was American. After deboarding the local bus from Puebla to Cholula I found the pyramid easily on foot. I focused on my mission, my backpack containing a phone and a camera and notebook to record my thoughts. I was excited to be working at last as a correspondent journalist—part of my dream come true. The other key, of course, was to locate my real dad. The town afforded several hotels, so I figured I could get a room in one of them for a few nights, until I completed the story of the pyramid and the local residents who lived there. I just hoped that my sketchy Spanish would get me by.

Chapter 19

Holding a map, I wandered aimlessly around the base of the pyramid. I refused to ask for help, since my Spanish wasn't that good, but needed to learn when the excavation on the pyramid began and other important historical facts. These facts would assist me in writing an informational feature article. I studied the map and the information on the reverse side of the pamphlet, which of course, was written in Spanish. I was hoping for illuminating insights—anything. People jostled by me, pushing me inadvertently along the sidewalk. I didn't see anything on the brochure to help, so I decided to start ascending the hundreds of steps leading to the top of the pyramid. I glanced up to the summit, on which a church structure perched. Slowly, I began the ascent, hoping to save my energy by not going too quickly. It took about twenty minutes to reach the pinnacle. At the top, I gazed around at the magnificent view of the city and surrounding hills. In the distance, I saw the looming mountain peaks of Popocatepetl and Iztaccihuatl. The latter, in English, was referred to as "White Woman" or "Sleeping Woman." The mountain supposedly resembles a woman lying on her back, often covered in snow. As I gazed into the distance, covering my good eye with my right hand, I could make out a shape that remotely resembled a sleeping woman. As I looked again at the brochure, I read that the first mountain in the distance, the one called "Popo" for Popocatepetl, was still an active volcano. There was a legend about both mountains. I pulled out the map once more and looked down at the section of pyramid that was exposed, wondering how to cover this for the paper. I had already taken many pictures, which was a start.

"May I help you?" a male voice asked in English. He spoke with a Spanish accent, I could tell. An attractive young man stood before me, smiling.

"Oh! Sorry. I was just startled that someone actually speaks English here. I've been hearing only Spanish all day."

The young man chuckled. "You might be surprised that many of us do speak English. One of our best kept secrets, perhaps." He appeared amused at his statement. "My name is Luis. Luis Mendez. And you are?" He waited patiently, while I found my voice.

"Uh, Casandra. But people call me Cassie. Cassie McMillen." I stumbled out the last name, hoping I wasn't being too forward to give it out so quickly. But he seemed so proper and polite. Luis was clean shaven, clean cut, with black wavy hair, the collegiate type, wearing a short sleeve, button down blue and plaid shirt and sharply pressed black slacks. I felt a bit underdressed at that moment, wearing a rumpled yellow tee over my baggy jeans. Slung over my right arm, my backpack kept sliding off during his introduction. I finally just set it down in front of me and looked around once more at the stunning view.

We walked around the perimeter of the pyramid at the summit, taking in the landscape from all 360 degrees. It was a clear day, so our sight stretched as far as the horizon. Luis made small talk about the area, and finally asked me where I was from and what brought me here to Cholula. I, in turn, found out that he was a medical student in his last year before interning at the university in Monterrey. His family lived in Puebla, and he was home visiting them for a week. We descended the long stairs after a half hour or so, the stairs zigzagging down in several switchbacks. The steps wound their way around the pyramid, and we paused at one point where the sign read that there once was an altar on that spot to sacrifice infants. I shuddered at that, and it suddenly occurred to me how my natural mother could have aborted me, since she was alone, an unwed mother, with nowhere to go for help. I thought about her possible confusion and hopelessness, but also her concern for me to grow up in a good home. Words from Claire from an earlier conversation when I was being critical of Stephanie echoed in my mind when she said, "I know that you can understand desperation. I'm certain that Stephanie went through that." It occurred to me while I stood at the pyramid, that my mother gave me life twice: the second time was when she made the decision to adopt me out. Maybe I was beginning to understand a little bit about her at last.

"Uh, Cassie, I asked you a question. Are you okay?"

"Wh-what? Sorry. I was thinking about something else."

"Well, I asked if you would join me for lunch at this little café nearby. We could talk more about the pyramid and the history of Cholula, if you want?" He let the question hang.

"Uh, sure. Yes. I need to eat someplace. Glad you know of a good place. I hope it's not too expensive."

Luis smiled again. "Nothing is too expensive around here, and the food is good."

As we entered the small café, strong spices and the aroma of simmering meat greeted us. I ordered the only thing I recognized on the menu: a plate of fish tacos. Luis ordered the café's specialty, a beef dish called Mixiote. The meat was wrapped in a cheesecloth and simmered in spices for hours. It was a delicacy, Luis explained to me.

While waiting for our orders, I asked, "Can you tell me more about the history of the pyramid, and perhaps the town of Cholula? What I read in Spanish is difficult to absorb. I took Spanish in high school, but it's been a while."

"Well, sure. I grew up in Puebla, which is just a few minutes away from here by bus. We all know the basics. The pyramid is supposedly the largest known pyramid in the world. Most of it is still buried in dirt, and thus, they are excavating it bit by bit. It is called, in English, The Great Pyramid of Cholula, or in Spanish, Tlachihualtepeti, which is Nahuati for "made by hand"."

"Wow. Wait. What is Nahuati?"

"The indigenous language, or dialect here of the Aztecs."

"And the largest known in the world? Are you sure? What about the Giza one in Egypt?"

"Well, look here at your brochure." Luis spread out the brochure in the middle of the table and pointed to a section. "It says here that it has a base four times larger than the one in Egypt but is hidden under a mountain. It has twice the volume of the Giza one, too." I followed his finger, reading the Spanish slowly, also noticing he had nicely manicured nails, cut short on his manly, light brown fingers. I became self-conscious of my own unkempt, jagged fingernails, noting to self to get a manicure somewhere in Puebla as soon as possible.

"So, tell me more about this large pyramid here." We read through the detailed brochure, as he translated each paragraph. I learned that the structure was built over time, beginning as early as 300 B.C., out of layers of adobe. The Aztecs used the pyramid as a temple for a thousand years before abandoning it for a smaller one nearby. With time, the pyramid was covered in layers of dirt and foliage, appearing as a mountain of sorts. The Spaniards didn't know of its existence, building the church at the top.

"That's an interesting point. I thought that they build the church on top of the pyramid on purpose."

Luis chuckled. "No, to the contrary. Cortes and his men had no idea about the pyramid when they arrived here in 1519. They destroyed the smaller temple nearby, erroneously assuming that to be the Aztec's only temple. Also," Luis paused for effect, running his finger over the information, "as you can see, they also massacred many people of Cholula. Historians say three thousand of them were killed in a single hour." Luis stopped to see my reaction.

I gasped at the huge number. "Oh my! Horrible!"

"Yes, truly. It goes on to say here that at least ten percent of the population was killed as well as many religious structures demolished. But the Spaniards never touched the pyramid because they never found it."

"Wow! Interesting."

"Yes. Right. It says something, don't you think?" Luis took another bite of his meal and folded the brochure on the table beside him.

"Yes, it does say something. The last joke was on the Spaniards, am I right?"

"I suppose so." Luis smiled ruefully, but then suddenly became somber. "But the Aztecs were the real losers." We continued eating in silence for a few minutes. Then, at one point, he prodded me more on my reasons for coming to Mexico.

"So," I replied, "my primary reason for coming to Mexico is to find my father. He studied the migration of Monarch butterflies at the university in Monterrey. I thought about going there first, to see if anyone had a record of his whereabouts there, but I figure he left there years ago. You see, he went there in 1987 and he hasn't been heard of, at least by those who knew him, in all that time." I looked down at my plate, my face feeling warm with embarrassment. Surely Luis must think me foolish to try to pick up such a cold trail.

Luis smiled pleasantly in my direction. He was sitting across from me in the quaint little Mexican restaurant. It was crowded and noisy, with voices all exuberantly speaking in rapid Spanish, and devouring their food with gusto. I missed the majority of what was said—they were speaking so fast— but they all said it so excitedly and happily. "I think that it is wonderful that you are trying to find your father. I don't blame you at all. Family is the basis of all our existence, don't you think?"

"Exactly. And I don't know what my father is like. I was adopted; I only discovered my real mother just a few years ago, and now she is dead. I hope to find him before it's too late." I felt better; he had validated my search for my father. I began to like this new friend Luis and dove into my lunch with renewed appetite.

Luis must have noticed because he went on. "Say, I will be going back to the university next week. With your permission I could try to see what I can find out about your father. Just give me his name, and anything else that would help. I could relay any information I find to you if you tell me your phone number. At least, I can probably find out more information than you since I am a student there and also fluent in Spanish. What do think?" He peered over at me as he took a bite of his Mixiote and flashed me a grin.

"Well, I guess that would be a good idea, I don't know...." I hesitated, realizing I had just met this guy.

"Before you decide, why don't you come on into Puebla and meet my parents and sisters?" I'll let them know you're coming, and Mom will prepare dinner. She will plan dinner anyway since I'm coming. It'll be great!" He must have sensed my hesitation and maybe a bit of fear. My bad experience on the island flashed back momentarily; I trembled inwardly, remembering. It was still a little too fresh in my mind. I paused, but finally nodded my head yes. I decided if I took the bus and met him there, it might be alright. I could always leave. It was just his family, and it would be during daylight hours. So, we set it up for two days from then, on a Wednesday. That would give me a little more time to look around in the picturesque Cholula town.

I walked the town alone the next day, observing the traditional adobe structures and cobbled streets. I noticed that there were countless churches in the city. I entered a few, spending a few minutes in them to take in the cool serenity, peace, and quiet in each. The churches were always open to everyone, unlike what I had noticed in the U.S., where they were unlocked only for services. But here, there were daily masses going on several times a day within each church. That struck me as amazing, as well as reverent. I stayed for a mass to see what transpired. Later, I found out that there were so many churches because the original intent of the Spaniards was to build a different church in Cholula for every day of the year. They did not quite reach that goal, but there were still many, in comparison to the size of the town.

Wednesday morning, I left the iconic city on a bus, with the address of Luis written down on a scrap of paper. I hoped I could figure out how to get to his house once I arrived in Puebla.

Chapter 20

It wasn't that difficult to find Luis's home. He had given me directions for which bus to take once I reached the main bus depot. I waited a few minutes for the correct transfer bus and rode for about fifteen minutes more to the stop he had told me to take. The locals stared at me on the buses just like before. I supposed that they don't see many American women riding one of their city buses alone. I refused to look directly back, and just stared out the window, taking in the sights of this impressive city of Puebla. It appeared historic and ancient. The main square of the city boasted a grandiose, towering cathedral. I read later that it was built the same as the cathedral in Mexico City, and at about the same time, when Cortes designed the town of Puebla as a colonial city in the 1500's. I noticed elegant buildings that interfaced with the cathedral, which Luis informed me were still used as city hall and other government offices.

The bus wound around the city's small, cobbled streets, and people jostled on and off at nearly every street. After a while, the bus entered a more affluent neighborhood, and it was soon my stop. I nearly overlooked it but saw the street sign, Manzanita Sur, in the nick of time. I jumped off and looked around. Most of the homes had wrought iron fencing either at their windows, around their properties, or both. It didn't look very welcoming. I sensed eyes peering out of their curtained and barred windows to see who had entered their neighborhood. A dog barked and a rooster crowed from the yard across the street, as if to greet me. I truly felt I was a "gringa" and out of my element here.

I was debating whether to wander down the street to my left, or go the other way, when out of nowhere, Luis appeared. "There you are!" he beamed, cutting across the street to greet me.

"Yes, I made it! Where do you live?" I looked around curiously, wondering which house was his family's.

"Actually, we live down the street a way," he said, pointing to the right. "It takes about a ten-minute walk." I slung my heavy backpack onto both shoulders to make the walk, but Luis intercepted it. "Here, let me carry that."

"Oh. It's okay." I felt embarrassed, but at the same time, relieved to have him take it. I had been toting that thing ever since checking out of the hotel earlier that morning. Luis insisted, so I let him carry it, and we trekked briskly to his house. I had to take double steps at times to keep up with him. From what I had observed, by Mexican standards, his two-story house was above average, with fresh yellow and red paint, and an uncluttered lawn. It too had the typical wrought iron bordering not only the property but at the windows and doors. The dry, crusty grass was mostly dirt, with an occasional shrub, but not much else. Dogs barked everywhere, and now and then I heard a rooster crowing again. I had noticed on our walk that homeowners kept chickens in their yards without even a shed or shelter for them. They seemed to just walk around in the yard at will. Apparently, Luis's house had neither chickens nor dogs. I was a little relieved, since I always had a fear of dogs or tall roosters rushing in on me, mouths open, poised to attack.

"We're here!" Luis grinned, holding the iron- barred door open for me to walk in. The door squeaked as he pulled it open. I felt like I was entering a prison or something. I stepped into a darkened hall, a bit hesitantly, not knowing at all what to expect. "Mama, Viv, Mercedes, we're here!" Suddenly, the three popped out from the kitchen, all smiles. The elder one ventured towards me while the sisters hung back.

"Welcome, welcome to our home," the woman said. "My name is Maria." Her English was perfect, although heavily accented. She shook my hand before giving me a small hug. She was petite, with graying short hair.

"My sisters, Viviana and Mercedes," Luis gestured to them, who also shook my hand and then gave the small, perfunctory hug. The sisters resembled one another very much, with Viviana being a little older looking than Mercedes. It appeared that Luis was the oldest sibling, but I wasn't sure. Both sisters had long, lustrous black hair, held back in bouncy ponytails. All three women wore aprons over slacks and excused themselves to go back into the kitchen. The aroma of simmering meat with spices wafted our way. "Our father will be home soon." I felt timid around this happy looking family; noticing their eyes resting on my frizzy hair, but they all kept smiling and invited me to sit in the living room. Only the younger sister looked behind her because of my wild eye. The room was attractively furnished in aging European-style furnishings. The effect was quaint and homey. The rose-colored sofa was supported on wooden feet and had buttoned back cushions. Classic prints decorated the walls, with a few family pictures as well. A television stood in a prominent spot, for easy viewing from the sofa and a green upholstered chair, also with a button back cushion. The floors were tiled, with oriental rugs. I observed later that tiled floors ran through the entire house. Soon there was a groan from the wrought iron door, and a man of roughly the same age as Luis' mother walked in. Luis stood up. "Here is my father, Esteban. The man glanced over at me, taking in my hair and weird eye in one swoop. "Papa, this is Cassie." The man grimaced a small grin and shook my hand. Without a word, he disappeared down the hall.

Luis sat back down with me on the sofa. "Papa works at the city hall. They have many pressures to deal with. He needs to change and get comfortable before dinner."

"Oh. Fine. No worry." I wondered at his father's curtness, but at dinner, Esteban seemed more relaxed and was the perfect host. The meal began with a Spanish wine, followed by a pasta soup. Maria took away the soup, reappearing with a main dish of simmered beef and vegetables. Small talk centered around Esteban inquiring about Mercedes' day at her private high school, Vivian's at the art school where she now attended and worked, and then about Luis at the university. All conversation was done in English, which I had not anticipated. I breathed a little easier, worried that I might feel left out if they used rapid Spanish. Spanish sounds so fast to English speakers perhaps due to the fact that it takes more words to convey the same meaning as English, which economizes on brevity of thought and contractions. Luis explained to me that they usually spoke Spanish in the home, but with an English-speaking guest, reverted to English.

"It's what we do. It's only polite to speak English if we have a guest who is an English speaker. Plus, it gives us a chance to practice it," he finished, his eyes focusing on me kindly.

Chilled canned pears, served in small dessert bowls, completed the meal, along with coffee, which Maria poured from a silver carafe. We drank from small China cups on saucers. The discussion suddenly turned to what brought me to Mexico, and I found myself having to explain to all of them about my search for my real father, and how I had finally landed a journalist correspondent position. They sipped their coffee politely, no one asking more questions about my journey here, until I stopped. The room grew quiet while the sisters helped Maria clear away the dessert bowls. I heard the fine China clink together as they picked up the dishes to carry to the sink. Esteban, Luis, and I stayed in our seats, still sipping coffee. Esteban refilled his cup and offered me more. I nodded, and he topped off my cup. Soon, Maria and the girls returned, and Maria was giving Esteban a look I didn't understand. He said something to her softly in Spanish—so softly I didn't pick up on it at all.

Esteban cleared his throat, and then stated in English, "Uh, we would all be honored if you would stay here with us while you are in Puebla. There is no need for you, a young American woman, to stay in a hotel."

"Yes, please stay with us," Maria added. "You can sleep in Viviana's room, and she can move to Mercedes' room. No problem." Maria smiled warmly, and the girls nodded in agreement, their ponytails bouncing in approval.

"Well, if you are sure. I will need to cancel my hotel reservation."

"It's all settled, then. Tomorrow, I'll take you on a tour around the city. Con permisso," Luis said to Maria, and stood up. I repeated that, stood up too, and we all retired to the living room to watch the evening news.

Chapter 21

I stayed in Puebla with the Mendez family two nights. I discovered that the city was intriguing as a colony of the Spaniards, but also had a diverse history as well. Many French and Italians settled there in its early years, as well as a Mid-Eastern group of people. All left their imprint on the city, and communities still thrived where those ethnicities were prevalent. Luis took me to lunch the first afternoon in the Italian neighborhood, and we were served by blonde waiters. I couldn't help but stare as our server brought out pasta and bread. Their complexions were so pale in contrast to the rest of the residents of the city.

Puebla, I learned, was the epicenter of the French and Mexican battle of Cinco de Mayo on May 5, 1862. The French Empire, under Napoleon III, outnumbered the Mexicans, but lost. Those who won served not only from the Mexican army, but also indigenous men from the surrounding small villages who showed up to fight with spears and machetes. The Mexican army was led by General Ignacio Zaragoza. The win was extremely memorable and remarkable, in contrast to the power of the French army. This fact boosted the morale of the Mexican people. I saw the statue, placed prominently in Puebla, to commemorate the Mexican heroes. The details of Cinco de Mayo are mostly lost on Americans living in the U.S., so I was surprised to discover more of the true story surrounding the event. I learned that many in the U.S. erroneously think that this date commemorates Mexican Independence from Spain. I looked up the correct date of independence from Spain, which is September 16.

All too soon it was time for me to leave and head out to the Monarch migration area to meet up with Claire and Preston. I wasn't sure if Preston's friend Tommy would be there or not. Before I boarded the bus Friday morning, Luis stole a swift kiss on my lips. "I promise I'll find out what I can when I return to the university on Monday." I felt his warm breath caressing my hair, and instantly, I regretted having to leave so soon. Luis clasped my hand and gave it a squeeze, gazing into my face tenderly. "Be careful. I'll call you soon."

"Okay, thanks." I was in shock from the kiss, and bounded up the steps of the bus, afraid to look back. I rode in silence, grateful for the empty seat next to me. I sipped on the complimentary mango juice and meditated on the last few days. I think I really like this guy, Luis. But why would he like me? I was confused but giddy. I grinned to myself and pulled out the notebook from my tour of Cholula and Puebla. I added a few notes regarding the battle of Cinco de Mayo, and then, a few comments to myself about Luis. I really did like him. Even his family seemed to like me for who I was, not even asking about my blind eye or glancing behind to see what I was looking at. Either they were very discreet or hadn't noticed. Either way, they made me feel welcome and accepted.

The ride took several hours, so to pass the time, I checked emails on my phone, which I had neglected to do since leaving the states. I opened one from a James Coburn, Atty. at Law. I was curious and a bit nervous as to what that could be concerning. It read:

Dear Ms. McMillen,
We have been assigned to take care of the affairs of a Dr. William Jordan. He has appointed me to manage his possessions since he is now in an assisted living facility in Lincoln City, where no pets are allowed. He listed you as caretaker for his cat, Dominican, should he have to

leave his home and move to an assisted living facility. I am writing to see if you are still able to fulfill this request. The cat is staying with his veterinarian until such time you can come to claim the animal. If you are unable to do so, the vet will then find a suitable home for the cat. Please advise your intention soon. If need be, the vet said he could foster the cat with a volunteer until such time you can arrange to pick him up. Thank you, James Coburn, Atty. at Law

The email included a phone number, but for now, I could at least email him back. I sat, stunned at the news. The last time I saw Dr. Jordan, he appeared fine and in good health, although he did comment that he was getting older. I wonder what had happened to make this change necessary. Poor Dominican. He probably feels abandoned. I wished that I could get him immediately, but here I was, down in Mexico, on some wild chase to find my father. My thoughts turned to what I should answer in the email. The email had been sent over a week ago, and I was reading it only now. I hope I wasn't too late for Dominican. I began my answer:

Mr. Coburn, Thank you for getting in touch with me. I am currently on a trip in Mexico and will return in about two weeks. I do indeed hope to take over the care of Dominican for Dr. Jordan, as I promised him I would some time ago. How is Dr. Jordan? I am concerned for his health, so please let me know. When I return to Corvallis, I will try to call you to arrange to pick up Dominican and hope to visit Dr. Jordan. I hope that will not be a problem for the vet or foster volunteer to care for the cat until then. Sincerely, Casandra McMillen

The bus lumbered on down the winding highway, and I peered out the window at the scrub brush on the hillsides, my mind racing at the turn of events in my life with Luis, and now Dr. Jordan and his cat. Then there was the whole reason for my being here—to find my father. My mind then visited the dark recesses of memory to the horrible date rape, and I struggled to maintain my composure, my breath coming in erratic bursts. I closed my eyes, willing myself to relax, and let the miles roll by, onward to the Monarch butterfly sanctuary. I remembered the spectacular sight of the butterflies on the island, forcing myself to imagine an even a more glorious sight in the mountainous terrain of Mexico. Hopefully, I would find my father waiting there, ready to embrace me into his life. I envisioned the photo Dr. Jordan showed of my father as a young man at the university. He would look older, for certain, perhaps with silver hair and a bit wrinkled around the eyes and mouth, but the warm, black- brown eyes and engaging smile would remain, summoning me with love. I just knew it. It had to be. The reason for my existence depended upon it.

With each passing mile, the anticipation increased, and I grew restless. I pulled out my notebook again and began putting together some ideas for my feature article. I was on assignment with my new correspondent job, after all.

Wind

Windows rattle, their frames hanging on tight

The bones of the house groan in protest

As the gusts lash out to claim victims.

Deck chairs yield, toppling off their porches

Foliage is rooted out, crumpled and lifeless.

Fir trees bend their heads,
lowering their great height,

while their arms snap off in despair,
plummeting to the earth.

Horizontal rains conspire with the relentless squall,

A lament for the winter, an unsparing hostility

for fauna, great and small, struggling to survive

until the warm summer sun returns once more.

Chapter 22

The hotel we had all chosen was located in the town of Ocampo, in the state of Michoacán. In tones of tan, Spanish adobe architecture struck entering tourists just as they had imagined, appearing as a travel brochure photo. It was near one of the four Monarch sanctuaries open to the public. The bus ride took two hours to Mexico City, where I transferred to the bus tour leading up to the sanctuary. That ride added an additional two to three hours. I wasn't sure since by then, I took a nap. Arriving in Ocampo, I got off and adjusted my backpack. I started walking, slowly taking in the new scenery. Maybe my father was here! I got a little excited, but tried to calm down, reasoning that it was only a small chance that he could be here. I reached the hotel, Villasenor, and checked in, using my broken Spanish. When I opened the door to my room that I would share with Claire, I collapsed onto one of the small beds. Two hours later, I heard a key in the door, and Claire's head appeared around the door, her red hair spiked up as usual.

"What a welcome sight you are!" I jumped up to give her a big hug. "Is Preston here too?"

"Yes! He got the same bus I did, so he's here too. Good to see you, Cass!" She grinned at me affectionately.

"So, did Tommy make it?"

"No, he couldn't get the time off."

The room was sparsely furnished, in need of paint, with two skinny beds and a table and chair. The window overlooked onto the street. Our bathroom was a shared one at the end of the hall. It would suffice; we were here on a quest—an adventure—and I had high hopes of finding at last, my father. We unpacked what we could and went downstairs to find Preston.

"Hey, ladies! Good to see you, Cass!" There was Preston, wearing his huge grin, already into a Corona at the small bar. He jumped up to give me a hug.

"Thanks for coming Preston. Don't know how I could keep going in my search without you guys."

"Wouldn't miss it for anything. This will be great fun! Take a seat and order something—my treat." Preston looked the same, with his straight, jet black hair and winsome smile. It was reassuring to be with friends again. We sat at the bar awhile, ordering Corona after Corona, catching up on one another's lives. Finally, we made our way into the dining room and ordered dinner, the only one menu option offered each evening, since the hotel was old and small. Tonight's entre was beef enchilada with rice and beans, a totally traditional Mexican meal. We discussed the coming morning, when our tour guide would take us to the sanctuary of the Monarchs on horseback. None of us was an experienced horseback rider but were determined to learn. I just hoped I would get a plodding and patient steed.

DAZZLING—SPECTACULAR—WERE THE ONLY WORDS THAT CAME to mind when we arrived in the Monarch wintering area at the top of the steep terrain. The butterflies clung to tree trunks but then, as the sun warmed their wings, they circled into the air, gently fluttering their iridescent orange and black wings, reflecting the sunlight. I drew in a sharp breath as I watched, mesmerized. The array in the breeze was breathtaking. There were hundreds—perhaps even thousands, in the atmosphere around us. We sat on our horses, in awe at the visual, the horses taking advantage of the moment to munch away obliviously on sprigs of grass. My horse, named Destiny, was a dapple grey, and fortunately, slow and patient. After a few minutes our guide, Juan, signaled us to dismount and open our packed lunches. Claire, Preston, and I didn't say much, just grinned and interacted when we could with the rest of the tour group. Ten of us comprised the group, but not all spoke English. Two Japanese students, a German couple, and three Spanish speaking young people completed the travel party. Juan spoke both English and Spanish, so all of us understood as he shared with us during the lunch. Meanwhile, the Monarchs continued to circle lazily overhead, creating a memorable moment for my mind to feast upon for years to come. So far, I saw no sign of my father. I half expected him to walk out to greet us. Perhaps, I reasoned, he had a cabin and lived here during the overwintering of the Monarchs. So, I ventured a question to Juan.

"Uh, Juan, have you by any chance seen a butterfly science guy up here, an African American? An older man? Anytime in the last few years?" I felt silly but had to ask the question. After all, I had come this far. I set my beef sandwich down on the wrapper, awaiting his reply.

"No, ma'am I don't think so. No one like that. Ever. Not many Americans make it up here, you know. The area isn't deemed very safe for American tourists." Juan appeared a bit embarrassed to say this, and looked down, focusing instead on his lunch. He took a bite of his sandwich, then got up to check on the tethered horses. I watched in silence as he withdrew a small bag of oats from his saddlebag and offered each horse a treat.

My heart sank. Nothing. I would check more in the town when we returned, but knew it was probably hopeless. Maybe Luis would come up with a lead at the university. Claire and Preston gave me a sympathetic look, but didn't say anything, continuing to eat their meal in silence. The other members of our group ate, talking softly in their own respective languages to one another.

As we mounted our horses and followed Juan and his tall bay horse back down the trail, I tucked the memory of the Monarchs, glistening in sunlight, into my mind for future reference. It was no wonder my father had devoted his life to studying them. They were a wondrous, natural phenomenon— unimaginable until one experienced them. One that a person would never tire of seeing. But where was my father? Why wasn't he here?

Chapter 23

We had just returned to Ocampo and said goodbye to our horses and our tour guide, Juan. Slowly, we shuffled back to our hotel which I only now noticed was covered in bougainvillea vines climbing up the crumbling adobe walls. Birds perched on the vines, calling out to me as I mounted the steps leading to the front door. It was as if the birds were mocking me. I was disappointed not to have found my father on our journey, even though I had hoped that to be the case. It wasn't to be that easy, I decided. I paused at the top step and turned around. As I surveyed the village, as I liked to think of it, I saw that it had a few shops to offer. I set off on foot the next day to see if my father just might appear from behind the counter in one of the small shops, or perhaps, someone knew of him. I still had time to search, since we planned to stay two more days. My limited Spanish would have to be sufficient as I made my way around the town and inquired about him.

As I entered a shop selling hardware and hiking supplies, I saw the back of a man reaching up onto the shelf for a box of nails. He had greying curly hair. I held my breath, waiting to see if when he spun around, it was my father. As he turned back to his customer with the box, I heard his fluent Spanish, and saw his face. No. Just an older and dark-complexioned Hispanic man. He glanced up at me a moment, as if to ask what I wanted, so I quickly began inspecting a flashlight within easy reach. Darn. False alarm. I was so hoping it would be that easy. The rest of the businesses held no promise of my father, nor did anyone I asked admit to having seen such a man. Maybe they didn't trust me to give out any concrete information. After all, I was just another American tourist invading their town.

Claire and Preston also searched but came up with nothing. All too soon, our time was spent, and we had to leave for Mexico City, and then take a flight home. It occurred to me on the way to the airport, that I might never learn of the whereabouts of Robert Harris, my father. He remained aloof and missing from my life as he always had from my birth. The reality of this hit me like a gut punch. I lost my appetite for the rest of the way back to the States.

My one solace in returning home without any leads on my father was Dominican. Dr. Jordan had been admitted into assisted living, and his cat awaited my arrival at the vet's office in Lincoln City. As I drove to the coastal town the day after arriving home in Corvallis, I excitedly anticipated bringing Dominican to my home. I would have my own cat at last! Dominican would always officially belong to Dr. Jordan, but I was adopting him. Just as I was once adopted. Suddenly, I had an insight into my adopted mom's life. Tully, too, may have been excited to receive me. Somehow, that idea had never occurred to me until now. Maybe I had been judging her a little too harshly, I finally admitted.

Before picking up Dominican from the vet, I stopped by the assisted living facility to visit Dr. Jordan. As I walked down the long hallway to his room, I went over the events in Mexico, deciding how much to share with Dr. Jordan. I decided that it depended upon his condition, so I would see how things went. I entered his room, and there he was, sitting upright in an easy chair, eating his lunch. He recognized me as I approached. "Casandra! How good to see you! Come on in and pull up that chair over in the corner," he said hospitably, motioning to the chair. I obeyed, retrieving the chair before I even said hi to him. He had a commanding but genteel manner even in this setting.

"Dr. Jordan! I'm so glad to see you, too! I just got back from Mexico yesterday, so I wanted to visit you as soon as I could and pick up Dominican." I grinned as I gave him a hug, and then sat down. "I will take good care of Dominican for you, don't worry."

Dr. Jordan chuckled. "I'm not worried in the least. Of all the humans besides me, he likes you the best. He will make a good companion for you."

"Oh, I know. I love that cat! We'll be good company for one another—unless I'm out on assignment or searching for my father." There. It was out. I still hadn't found him.

"Oh? No luck then? Well, what do you suppose? But did you see the butterflies in Mexico while they were wintering there?"

"Yes. It was spectacular! We rode to the sanctuary by horseback and had a guide and everything. It was so awesome there!"

"But no Robert Harris, I presume?"

"No. Not a trace. I was so disappointed. I felt optimistic that he was living at the sanctuary in a rustic cabin or something. I guess the search is harder than I expected it to be." I looked down at my hands, trying to hold back a few tears.

Dr. Jordan must have noticed, as he reached over and patted my hands reassuringly. "There, there. Don't fret. You will go back again one day and try in another location. I know you will find him eventually." He smiled tenderly at me before going on. "In the meantime, take good care of my Dominican for me. When you return to the sanctuary in Mexico, just find a suitable cat sitter."

Of course, I will, Dr. Jordan. Don't' worry. I am so excited to have Dominican come to live with me! And we will keep in touch. Do they allow pets to visit you here? I could bring him sometime."

"Well, dear, I'm not sure. You would have to check at the front office. But it's okay if not. It would be a long trip for Dominican to come from Corvallis to see me here. Don't worry about that." He looked sad as he said this, so I knew it was a great effort for him to lose Dominican.

Before long, it was time for his therapy, so I said my goodbye, with promises to call soon and let him know how Dominican had settled in with me. I drove straight to the vet's, anticipating my little traveler to ride back home in my car. I would need to buy food and litter for him, since I had no time to prepare ahead since arriving from Mexico. Would Dominican remember me?

Chapter 24

Dominican greeted me at the vet's with purrs and brushed up against my legs, winding himself around me countless times. The tech on duty rounded him up and crated him in his carrier. I thanked everyone and carried my new roommate, Dominican, out to my car. He meowed only for the first five minutes on the ride to Corvallis, and then seemed to settle down for the rest of the nearly two-hour ride to my apartment.

Dominican adjusted to his new life with me easily, seeming to understand that this was what Dr. Jordan had in mind for him. He was a perfect pet. We developed a routine, with his feeding times corresponding to my mealtimes at breakfast and dinner. From the first night, he slept at the foot of my bed.

We enjoyed this tranquil pace for a month until I got the call from Luis in Mexico. "So, Cassie, I found out from the university that when he left there, he intended to live and research in the Sierra Chinua, near Angangueo, in the state of Michoacán. You didn't go there, right?"

"No, I didn't. We went to the sanctuary out of Ocampo. For some reason, I thought that was going to be the place where I'd find him. But obviously, I was wrong." My heart raced, just at the thought of actually finding my father. I could already picture our sweet reunion, just like out of a movie. He would look up to see me, blink a moment, and then rush to take me into his arms, and say how he always dreamed of meeting up with me, his daughter.

"Cassie, Cassie, are you listening? I asked you when could you go there? I could arrange to meet you there and we could look for him together."

"Oh, sorry. I was daydreaming of what it will be like when I see him. Really? Would you do that? Could you meet me there? I would like that very much. I don't think my friends are up to another wild chase just yet."

"Sure. Just let me know when you can do it, and I'll be there. No problem. I can work on my research online from anywhere. Don't have to be on campus this semester. In fact, I was going to go home to Puebla and work from there. I can just as easily meet you at that Monarch sanctuary."

"I have to arrange for Dominican, Dr. Jordan's cat, first. I'll get back to you."

After we hung up, I thought about what to do. I knew a friend from Oregon State who needed a place to stay. When I called Joan to ask if she would cat sit at my apartment, she was more than happy to do so. Next, I had to arrange at the newspaper to be on assignment in Mexico again. I figured if they agreed, I could accomplish two things at once: work and finding my father.

Chapter 25

February 2011

I decided to wait until the following winter for the next Monarch over-wintering season to ensure better odds of finding my father. Even though my university friend, Joan no longer needed a place to live temporarily, she agreed to cat sit Dominican. I departed Portland and met Luis at the airport in Mexico City; and from there, we planned to board the tour bus bound for Angangueo together. Nervously, I gave Luis a quick hug. He pecked me on the cheek, and I felt my face growing hot. Somehow, Luis again made me feel that way as I quickly realized that I had missed him. His grin said volumes as we affectionately fixed our eyes on one another before grabbing our luggage and walking out of the terminal to the awaiting bus. "Cassie, I missed you."

"Yeah, me too."

"So, let's just enjoy this adventure together, right? Even if we don't find your father, we can have fun. I needed a vacation."

"Right. We'll be optimistic but enjoy the trip regardless."

'That's the spirit," Luis said as he squeezed my hand tenderly. Just his touch sent a quick spark up my arm. He beamed at me and took my elbow as we boarded the tour bus.

After we stowed our bags and were sitting comfortably next to one another on the soft, grey upholstered seats, I had to ask, "Why did you really agree to meet me for this trip back to the Monarch sanctuary?" I gazed up at his face, searching for the truth in his eyes. They were unreadable.

"Well, to be honest, I thought you needed some support. You are undertaking a daunting task, to be sure. It isn't all fun and games. Plus, I know the language better, since Spanish is, after all, my first language. Aren't you glad for me to be here?" Luis feigned an injured expression.

"Uh—of course! Yes—really glad you are here. Thank you." I looked down, embarrassed at having to say that. Luis chuckled, then took my hand. He held it, not saying anything. We both simply stared out the window at the passing scenery until a steward walked through with juice or soda options and packaged cookies. Relieved for the interruption, I took a Sprite and some butter cookies. Luis did the same, our hands letting go to hold onto the refreshments.

The miles flew by, and we arrived about two hours later at the small village of Angangueo, near the butterfly sanctuary. The tour bus pulled up in front of an inn, ancient and obviously in decay. The stucco was crumbling while ivy climbed up the sides of the building just as the other inn, a year prior, in the other mountain village. The town looked hot and dry, but also exotic for me, an American, now from the State of Oregon. Luis and I each grabbed our own bags and headed in. We checked into separate rooms which faced one another on the second floor. There was a single, small bathroom with a bathtub at the end of the hall, and the rooms were sparce but comfortable. Each afforded a small bed, a chair and table, and a window overlooking the street below.

"Meet you downstairs in the café in thirty minutes?" Luis asked brightly.

"Sure." I glanced around the small room, deciding where to set my bag. I threw it onto the bed and dug out a fresh pair of denim shorts and sleeveless shirt. I dressed quickly, checked my hair in the tiny mirror hanging by the door. There wasn't much I could do about my frizzy hair. Since I was early, I walked outside to survey the little town for a few minutes before waiting for Luis in the hotel's café.

I observed Luis as he entered the small café. He seemed so perfectly at ease, smiling and nodding at the waiter, speaking briefly to him in Spanish. I was indeed fortunate to have Luis here with me. He seemed to pave the way, creating warmth and inspiring trust to those we encountered. I would need that in order to inquire about my father's whereabouts. Luis' eyes lit up when he saw me saunter over to his table. "There you are. What will you have?" Luis stood and pulled up the chair for me to sit. I felt awkward suddenly— no man had ever done that for me before.

"Uh, I don't know. I'll have what you get I guess." At that, Luis spoke to the waiter quickly in Spanish. I recognized the words "sparkling mineral water."

"Cassie, remember that I told you that the university informed me that your father was last known to have come here, to this particular butterfly sanctuary and town. I think we have a good chance of finding him here." He leaned over, grasping my right hand. We sat across the small table from one another, our hands touching in the center of the table, until the waiter brought our mineral waters in clear glass bottles. Relieved, I let go of his hand to pick up my bottle, touching it to my lips for a sip. It was tepid— room temperature.

"Ugh. I was expecting a cold beverage to quench my thirst." I made a face and set the bottle down.

"Hey, what did you expect out here in the wilderness? Tastes great!" Luis took a big swig off his bottle, setting it down with emphasis, grinning back at me.

"Well, next time I'll be expecting the warm flavor."

Fly Home, Butterfly

Luis laughed, then fastened his gaze on me. "Let's plan our strategy for finding your father, okay?"

"I like your confidence, Luis. Let's make this day count." Luis instilled a reassurance I didn't have. He helped push me forward to my purpose for being here again. We finished our mineral water and headed over to the small building which housed the tours to the butterfly sanctuary and signed up for the early morning trip on horseback. While it was still a business day in the town, we wandered from shop to shop, Luis inquiring for an American professor who may have come here in search of the Monarchs. Everyone shook their heads or averted their eyes, refusing to give any information despite Luis' command of Spanish. I felt a sense of depression. Why didn't at least someone know something about my father?

"It's okay. We go to the sanctuary tomorrow. Who knows what we will find there? I have hope. Don't worry." Luis grabbed my hand as we strolled back to the hotel for a simple meal of rice, beans, and tortillas. "Let's get some good night's rest. We have a long day tomorrow, right?" Luis grinned, trying to be the positive one. At the door to my room, he pecked me on the cheek, slowly letting loose of my hand. Quickly, I opened my door and entered, closing it softly. I heard Luis whistle as he unlocked his own room and enter. I didn't understand my feelings at this point. I wanted to sing yet felt disappointed that no one so far had seen an American man wandering around in search of migrating butterflies. So why did I feel this surge of happiness—an indecipherable warmth? Confused but content, I undressed and fell into bed and into a fitful sleep, marked by dreams of endless searching for my father. Around two in the morning, I awoke with a start, dreaming that I had found him high on a mountaintop. He smiled and embraced me, but I was crying.

Chapter 26

We left the village early the next morning before sunrise. The mountain air chilled me so that my teeth chattered. The bay horse I was riding plodded behind Luis' chestnut, a more spirited horse who strained at the bridle. Luis skillfully kept him in line, and we formed a long procession behind the guide. Our seasoned guide, Jose, appeared to be around thirty-five, dark and weathered from endless days in the saddle. He wore a wide-brimmed hat and sat easily in the saddle of a dapple-gray gelding, which was obviously used to taking the lead. Jose set out, reining his horse to a slow pace, allowing for the caravan of adventure seekers behind him, eight of us in all. I asked myself why I was attempting this yet again. It seemed pointless. Even the villagers had no recollection of my father ever being here. Then Luis turned around, giving me an encouraging grin, his left thumb up to signify support. I had to smile back. He was right—I had to have hope. Maybe today would be the day.

Mile after mile the horses trudged forward, their heads bent low when they encountered the numerous steep slopes on the narrow stone laden trail. I felt sorry for them. They had to perform this thankless task nearly every day, and for what? Their food and a stable at the end of the day. At one point, my horse stumbled on a large rock, and I caught my breath. The horse quickly recovered his balance, and we continued onward. The other riders behind us chatted amicably; they must all know one another, I concluded. Our guide was silent, as were Luis and I, who followed directly behind him. The scenery around us was breathtaking; tree limbs overhanging above us, some so low that we could touch them as we passed by, and birds singing as dawn broke on the dank, morning air. Still the horses climbed upward towards the sanctuary.

We reached a clearing where the guide stopped and motioned for the rest of us to do likewise. "Here the horses take a rest. Please dismount," he commanded in English, his accent thick but understandable. He then showed us how to tether our horses before pulling out from his saddlebag our sandwiches. I saw some riders getting sandwiches from their own saddlebags. All of us sat on the ground under a tree in a circle of sorts, quietly eating or chatting softly. Overhead, the sun rose higher, and the birds became silent, anticipating a hot afternoon. Soon, we were told to mount our assigned horses, and were again slowly ascending the mountainside. I felt anxious, and a twisted knot of hopelessness formed in my stomach. Luis turned around as if reading my mind, giving me a wide grin. I drew in a deep breath. Slowly, we moved on.

Two hours later, we arrived in a clearing. There, butterflies circled slowly overhead, a dazzling array of orange and black, set against the sunny blue sky. Our guide Jose motioned for us to dismount once again and tether our horses. As we did so, I noticed the butterflies hanging onto tree branches and trunks in huge clusters. Before I looked away from the breathtaking scene on the trees, there, partially hidden, was a small cottage. A fence surrounded the small house, trimmed by bright yellow flowers. In the back was a well-tended vegetable garden. The home appeared occupied, with curtains to the windows and a chair and table on the front porch. At that moment, I gasped. A tall, older black man with salt and pepper hair emerged from the cabin and stepped onto the porch. He held a book in one hand and a glass of wine in the other. He placed the wine glass on the small wooden table next to the chair and sat down. "Luis," I whispered loud enough for him to hear, "Do you see what I see?"

"Yes, but the question should be, 'Do you see who I see?'" Luis added.

My heart was pounding. Could my search for my father be ending here at long last? Could it really be true? Way up here on a mountainside in Mexico? It seemed surreal. My legs wobbled, partly from riding horseback for hours, but also from this possible new revelation. The man on the porch seemed unconcerned by our tour group arriving, ignoring us all, settling in for a good read. A large dog, perhaps a golden retriever, lumbered from around the back of the cottage and barked, but the man softly commanded the dog to be quiet. The dog obediently stopped barking and sat down beside him, wagging his tail. The man spoke to the dog in English— that much I heard. My heart quickened even more.

The others in our group gave the man a curious stare before averting their eyes, and then quietly wandered around the clearing, snapping photos, speaking in murmured tones, afraid to frighten away the butterflies. Jose announced that we would rest our horses for an hour, and we were free to roam the area, enjoying the thousands of butterflies of the sanctuary. I felt so overwhelmed, not just at the sight of the Monarchs, but of course, at the prospect that this man on the porch might be my lost father. But how to proceed? "Luis, what do I do? I—uh, can't just walk up and ask if he is my father." Suddenly, the whole idea of all this searching was absurd—ridiculous even. What was I thinking? Luis paused, trying to decide how to advise me, when we observed Jose waving to the man on the porch. The man waved back in return.

My answer revealed itself. "There you go. Ask Jose to introduce you, Cassie."

"Are you sure? I feel shy suddenly." It seemed crazy. How could I have stumbled upon my real father up here in the middle of nowhere? The likelihood seemed impossible.

"What if he is my father but won't admit it?"

Luis sighed. "Yes, that is possible. You knew that from the beginning of your search. But you have to try, right? Ask Jose. That's why we came here, remember?" Luis grinned encouragingly, pushing on my back gently. I reluctantly walked over to where Jose sat on the grass by his horse, sipping on a bottle of water. I crouched down close to where he sat and tried to speak. The words caught in my throat, and I just looked at him for a moment, my mouth refusing to say the words.

"Yes, you have a question about the butterflies?" Jose continued eating his sandwich and surveyed me curiously, awaiting my question.

"Um, not so much about the butterflies. It's—it's about the man you just waved to. Do you happen to know his name?"

"Why do you ask? Everyone comes up here to see the butterflies, not the person who lives in a cabin. But yes, I know his name." Calmly, Jose finished his sandwich, wiped his mouth with his sleeve, and waited.

"Well, um, he looks like someone I might know."

Jose chuckled. "I get that all the time. People think they know someone but always it's just something that reminds them of someone. But no harm to ask his name. He goes by "Bob."

My breathing stopped. My heart did a flip. "Th—thank you. Would you—uh, could you, introduce me to him?"

"Well, that I'm not so sure about. You see, he lives up here to observe the butterflies, and also, to remain alone. I respect that. He pays me to bring his supplies and mail every week and all, but socializing is something I will not impose upon him." I must have looked disappointed, so he added, "sorry."

"Oh. Okay. Thanks anyway." I rose slowly, feeling a bit taken back. Dejected, I trudged back to where Luis sat, and whispered that Jose had rejected my request.

"That's fine. I'll go with you over to the cottage, and we will meet him together. Come on, Cassie," Luis immediately stood, and took my arm. I felt as though I were going to my execution instead of possibly meeting my birth father. What do I say? What will he say?

"Who did you say you were?" Bob looked up at me sharply, taking in my blind eye and staring at it a moment before turning to my good eye after I introduced myself as Casandra McMillen. His eyes seemed to bore through me as I repeated my name.

"No, I don't know a Casandra McMillen. You must be mistaken. I don't know who you are." He went back to his book reading after taking a sip of the red wine, setting the glass down gingerly.

I looked over to Luis for help. At that moment, he was feigning interest in the myriad of fluttering butterflies circling overhead. "Well, did you once know a woman by the name of Stephanie Hoffman?" At the mention of my mother, Bob's eyes flickered in recognition, and he sputtered, spewing wine onto the floor of the porch. He appeared flustered and set the book down on the table roughly, nearly tipping over the wine.

"I think this conversation is over." He rose, preparing to return inside the cabin.

"Wait! Please!" Luis propelled into action. "Cassie, or Casandra, came all this way to meet you! Please give her a few minutes of your time. Please," he pleaded.

"Why should I do that?" Bob said, his face a cold, emotionless mask.

"Be—because, you are my father!" I blurted out. "Look at me! I look a lot like you, don't I? I have spent my whole life trying to figure out who I am and why I am the way I am. And Stephanie, my biological mother, passed away last year, by the way. I can't ask her anything more now. She's dead."

Bob blinked momentarily at the news that she had died, and then stared at me like he had seen a ghost. "My condolences. I have nothing further to say to that. Go away and leave me alone." He spun on his heels and disappeared into the cabin, firmly shutting the door behind him. I heard the lock turn. The glass of wine and book lay on the table, the only evidence that I had finally met the man who was my father, here before me, just moments ago. I stood at the bottom of the porch, and then mounted the four steps leading to it. I picked up the book and read the cover. It was entitled, *Overwintering of the Monarchs* by Robert Harris.

"Luis, why would he be reading his own book?" It was then that I also noticed the small notebook and pen lying on the table. I picked it up, reading the notations of the notebook. "Oh, now I think I see. It says, 'revisions to the second edition.' I guess he is preparing to publish again, with new observations. Hmm."

"Yes, it seems that your father is a true scientist. Always reconfirming his work," Luis said gently. "He loves his work above all else I suppose."

"No room in his life for his own daughter." My voice wavered as I said the words. There were no liquid tears this time; only dry, unshed ones that I sensed welling up from behind my eyes. Luis reached for my hand just in time to catch me before I stumbled down the steps of the cottage porch.

Chapter 27

February 2011

I felt heartsick as we rode down the mountain in silence. After searching for two years and traveling countless miles, I manage to find my real father, only to have him reject me as well as refusing to acknowledge my deceased mother. I wished now that I had not undertaken this arduous quest. It had merely led to even more grief and disappointment. At least in my mother's case, she had redeemed herself with the poignant letter and photos she had willed to me. In her letter, I recalled now, she had explained her love for me and her decision for giving me up for adoption. This man—this Robert Harris—was a cold, calculating scientist who had no room in his life for either the mother of his child or his own daughter—me. I had been dismissed out of hand before I was born, sight unseen. From the information that I was able to glean, he had left for Mexico before I was born, and vanished. Somehow, I made the ridiculous mistake of thinking that he might be excited and happy to finally meet me, his own daughter. Now I understood that it was all purposeful—he never wanted to meet me—I had intruded upon him on this remote mountaintop of a butterfly sanctuary.

Silently, our tour group, mounted on our horses, trailed behind our guide, Jose, winding down the steep mountainside. The horses plodded along behind his lead horse, snorting every so often in protest. I felt so dejected that my horse must have sensed my despair—and that my mind was distracted in thought. Abruptly, he bolted off the trail and into the thicket, rearing up on his hind legs. It caught me off guard; I wasn't hanging onto the saddle horn, so I fell off. The horse lunged farther into the undergrowth, and pandemonium broke out. The other horses reared, neighed, and snorted. Jose jerked to a stop and dismounted, grabbing a first aid kit from his saddlebag. I just lay on the ground on the side of the path, moaning in pain; Luis was already at my side to help me. The rest of the party were yelling and attempting to reign in their unruly horses, finally coming to a halt near Luis' horse. Jose knelt, checking me over. "I have a first aid kit right here. Let's see— where does it hurt, Cassie?"

"Ooo. Hurts here," I said, holding onto my left elbow with my right hand.

"Here?" Jose said, gently touching my left elbow.

"Oww, yes. There."

"Okay. I have an ace bandage to hold it in place until we get down from here. There is a physician in the town who can help you. You are lucky that your horse didn't trample you."

"It's going to be okay, Cassie," Luis added, who by now held my head on his lap, trying to comfort me as well.

"But you have to get back on your horse. Just show the horse you are the boss, and keep him reigned in, okay?"

I realized I had no other choice. "Uh—okay. I will try."

One of the other women in the group called out, "You can do it, Cassie. We will help you from behind so your horse stays in line." Others agreed, joining in to encourage me. Everyone clapped as I remounted my horse, and soon, we were on our way down the mountain again. I gripped the reins tighter with my good hand and tried to focus. Every step the horse took jarred my injured elbow, and I winced in pain. At least, for the time being, it took my mind off the bitter disillusionment of encountering my father.

THE DOCTOR WAS AWAITING OUR GROUP AT THE STABLE, READY to assist me immediately. Jose had contacted him when we got within range of his phone. After giving me a cursory check, the doctor asked Luis and me to follow him to his office for treatment. Luis took my good arm, and I slowly hobbled to the doctor's office. I felt a pain in my left leg by now and it hurt to walk. Inside the small office, the doctor surmised that my elbow was sprained but not broken, and wrapped it carefully, giving me a sling to wear for the next couple of weeks. My leg was just bruised, according to him. I was shaken, but grateful that it was only a sprain not a fractured bone. We returned to the stable to speak with Jose. He was still there, brushing down and feeding the horses. "Uh, Jose," I hesitated, "could I speak to you a moment?"

"Certainly. Go ahead. Itchy here won't mind if you talk while I brush him."

"Itchy?" The horse was a beautiful white with grey dapple on his coat. *How could he get such a mundane name?* I wondered.

Jose seemed to read my mind. "Yeah, he got that name because he loves being scratched behind his ears. Go ahead. He loves it."

I tentatively reached out my hand and scratched his left ear. As I did so, Itchy cocked his head toward me, begging for more. So, I continued to gently stroke Itchy's ears, and prepared my mind for what to say. Luis watched from a distance, observing the other horses in their stalls as they crunched on hay. I decided to just blurt it out. "So, uh, the man at the cottage is my father." Jose stopped the brush midair, turning to look at me full on.

"Oh. Why didn't you say so while we were up there? I had no idea. I would have introduced you had I known that."

"Well, I had to meet him first to be sure. But he is. I'm certain of that now. It's a long story, but I have been looking for him for a couple of years but have never met him until today." I tried to keep my composure, but it was difficult. I had been through a lot today, emotionally as well as physically. I felt my eyes tearing up a bit. I sniffed loudly to get control, and then continued. Luis stepped closer and took my hand to lend support. "I was wondering if I could get his mailing address and give you mine to share with him someday. I mean, if it's okay with you, that is."

Jose resumed his brush strokes, using long, even movements as if to have a moment to consider how to respond. The smooth, quiet brushing sound was calming as I waited. Itchy leaned in as Jose brushed his neck. "Yes, I suppose I could do that. Perhaps with time, your father will reach out to you. At least, you will have given him a way to contact you. Yes, that would be good. He has the option to do so or not."

"Oh, thank you so much, Jose. I really appreciate that. Here. I'll just give you my business card from the newspaper I work for. It has a mailing address, my email, and my cell phone number." I handed him the card before continuing. Jose glanced at it, and then shoved it in his shirt pocket. "We loved the tour, by the way, didn't we, Luis?" Luis grinned and nodded. "Since I am a journalist, I took photos to take back to my newspaper. I do feature stories. May I include a photo of you? If so, I just need you to sign a permission form. Standard procedure."

"I would be honored," Jose said, bowing in mock deference. He signed my form as we laughed jovially, and at last, said our goodbyes. I limped slowly back to our hotel, Luis holding onto my good arm. My left leg was bothering me, so we took our time. The doctor had tested the leg, having me stand on it, and wasn't overly concerned. In such a remote village, the physician had no way to do x rays to be certain. Each step was painful, so I didn't feel like talking—Luis must have taken the cue and said nothing.

Tediously, I took each step of the stairs slowly, finally arriving to my room. "I think I need to lie down for a while. I'm really worn out."

"Sure, Cassie. I'll check on you in an hour or so. Maybe we can get a bite to eat then, and just relax for the evening. He unlocked my door for me before turning to go to his own room. I gave him a weak smile and shut the door. I gingerly stretched out onto the bed, and only then allowed the tears to unleash. It was such a crushing blow to be unwanted by my other parent—my own father. Silently, so I wouldn't worry Luis across the hall, I wept, smothering the tears in my pillow.

Much later, I heard a soft knock on my door. "Cassie, it's me. Luis. May I come in?"

"Uh, okay. What time is it?" Groggy, I stumbled to the door to unlatch the lock. I must have finally fallen asleep.

"Oh, about six o'clock. It's been a couple of hours. I've been strolling through the village, waiting for you, and I found these." Luis pulled out a bouquet from behind his back. It was full of assorted summer flowers in red, orange, yellow and pink, tied with a red bow and nestled in a vase of water. He grinned sheepishly.

"Oh, Luis! How nice!" I felt embarrassed, not knowing what to say. No man had ever given me flowers before. I reached out to take them and set them on the empty table. "They're beautiful, Luis."

"I think you need these today. It's been a hard day for you."

"You're right about that. Oh, my elbow really hurts now. And my leg."

"Let's get you some aspirin or something down the way at the little store, okay? Then we'll order something to eat."

"Sure. Just let me freshen up a bit. I'll meet you downstairs in about twenty minutes?"

Chapter 28

Since it hurt me to walk, Luis ran down to the corner store and bought some aspirin. We decided to save my steps and eat dinner in the hotel. I met him there after changing into a fresh, yellow blouse and black, cotton capris. Luis arrived at my table with aspirin in hand, and something else concealed in a small, brown paper bag. "What's in that?" I quizzed, after swallowing two aspirins. I stared at the bag after he placed it on the table next to his left hand.

"Oh, I'll show you in a bit. Let's order first." His eyes danced. He looked like a young boy with a secret he wasn't allowed to share.

"Well, okay then. If you'll show me soon. Otherwise, the mystery is too much," I teased playfully. Our server appeared at our table, and we ordered a glass of chardonnay for each of us. To save time, we also put in our order for our meal, two plates of their special, which was shredded beef tamales on a bed of rice. We ordered salads on the side. As we sipped our wine, making me heady right off due to the aspirin, Luis withdrew something from the mystery bag. Obviously hand crafted, it was a silver butterfly on a beaded necklace. I gasped. "Oh, Luis, it's beautiful! Is it for me?" I was incredulous; no guy had ever given me anything, let alone an item of jewelry.

Luis chuckled. "Of course, it's for you. Here. Let me put it on you." He got up from his chair and went behind mine to place the necklace around my neck and clasp it shut. I shivered as I felt his fingers brush lightly on my neck. I reached up to feel the butterfly with my good hand. The necklace rested on my neck as if it belonged there.

"Luis, I love it! Thank you! But why did you do this? You just bought me flowers today too." I was perplexed. What did it all mean?

Luis sat down across from me and took my right hand. My left, of course, was strapped to the sling by my side. "What it means, Cassie, is that I'm falling in love with you." He smiled tenderly and watched for my reaction. I was stunned—speechless.

"But—but why? Why me?" I didn't know what to say. My defenses had carried me this far in life, and here I was, perhaps in a love relationship that I didn't know what to do with.

"Cassie—I love you. I have loved you since the moment we met on top of that pyramid in Cholula. I've been patiently waiting for the right time to tell you." He hesitated before continuing, lowering his eyes. "I'm hoping, that by this time, you love me too." He looked past me, to the window behind my chair, fearing that perhaps, it wasn't the right time yet. Perhaps he was rushing me.

"Oh, Luis, I don't know what to say. You know my past, that I was adopted, and I have been searching for my biological parents, I suppose to discover my identify. While searching on South Padre Island, something horrible happened. Nothing can erase that. Someday, I will tell you more about it. I—I don't know what to feel anymore." I looked down into my lap, thinking that I was the most pathetic girlfriend anyone could ever have.

"It's alright, Cassie. You will heal with time. They say that time is a great healer." He knew not to pressure for more information. He reached higher, holding gently to my good arm, and continued. "Cassie, do you think you could love me just a little?" At that moment, our server arrived with our salads. Awkwardly, I cleared my throat, withdrawing my arm from the table so that there was room for the plates. Silently, we both picked up our forks and picked at the lettuce.

I set the fork down, clearing my throat again before answering Luis. "Yes, I could love you. Maybe I already do; I just am confused right now. I've been confused, actually, for years. But I never thought a man like you would say he loved me." I sighed before continuing, collecting my thoughts. "Yes—yes! I'm sure I love you. I'm afraid, though. Do you understand anything about that?" I implored him with my eyes, not knowing how he could possibly understand.

"Cassie, I will never hurt you. I will always love you, and I want to be in your life always."

"But how? You live in Mexico, and I live in Oregon, the U.S.A. How is that ever going to be possible?"

Luis smiled and took my hand again. "Cassie, with love, anything is possible. I'm certain. Here's the deal. I can visit you on a travel visa, and we can see how things go. What I'm hoping is that you will agree to marry me some day. Will you marry me, Cassie?"

I felt tears falling on my cheeks, not understanding why. "Are you sure, Luis? I do love you; I just don't understand love yet."

"I've never been so sure of anything in my life. My family loves you, too. They keep asking me when I'm going to pop the question."

"Oh, Luis, yes. Yes, I will marry you if you are patient with me. I just need a little time to sort it all out." I smiled through the tear droplets that fell onto my lap. After eating Luis walked me up the stairs, taking my good arm, and we strolled back to our rooms. At the door to mine, he hesitated.

"Cassie, may I kiss you?" Not waiting for my answer, he bent close, kissing me lingeringly on my lips. I felt myself returning the kiss. Finally, he broke it off, smiling sheepishly. "I wish for more, but that's okay. We'll take it slow, alright?" With that, he took my key from my hand and opened my door. "Goodnight, Cassie." I gave him a longing look, and softly shut my door.

Never in my wildest imagination did I think I would find my father only to lose him and gain a man who proposed to me, all in the same day. It was a bittersweet moment. I needed time to process it all.

OUR FLIGHTS HOME WERE SCHEDULED FOR TWO DAYS FROM NOW, so we took it easy at the hotel in order for my injuries to heal. At the airport, we said our goodbyes. He would go back to Monterey to finish his term at the university, and I, to Oregon. Back to my job and Dr. Jordan's cat, Dominican. As I sat at the gate awaiting departure, I began searching through my emails on my phone, since there was plenty of wi-fi at the Mexico City airport. It was then my eye caught a message from Dr. Jordan's attorney. I read through quickly, then reread to be certain I understood.

Dear Ms. McMillen,

I regret to inform you that my client, Dr. Wilbur Jordan, passed away on February 24. I am handling his estate, which lists you as sole heir. Dr. Jordan had no children or wife, and specifically listed you to receive his entire estate, including his home in Lincoln City, pending probate. When you read this, please contact my office.

My condolences,

James Coburn, Atty. at Law.

I was stunned. I thought Dr. Jordan was doing okay, or so I thought. The loss shook me. I sat there, oblivious as the airline steward called out the row numbers for boarding. Finally, I heard my name over the intercom— they had finished boarding all passengers except for me. Startled, I jumped up and grabbed my carryon, and wended my way to the boarding area.

Chapter 29

The flight home was a blur. In my mind, all I could see was dear, sweet Dr. Jordan and Dominican sitting together in the living room of the little beach bungalow. I had visited Dr. Jordan a couple of times since he had relocated to assisted living, but during those visits he still seemed sharp and vibrant. I missed little Dominican but would see him soon in my apartment. Now Dr. Jordan was gone—another loss. He had become like a dear grandfather to me. I was shocked when James Coburn, the lawyer, said that Dr. Jordan had willed me his estate, including his home. Tears moistened my cheeks just as a stewardess brought me the hot tea I ordered. She looked at me, and gently set it down on my tray. "Sometimes it is hard to leave a loved one, isn't it?" She smiled sympathetically.

"Yes—yes, it is." Chagrinned, I realized that she was referring to leaving someone behind before travel. It was then that I allowed my mind to recall Luis. Yes, it was hard to leave him. My mind swirled, making me dizzy, so I leaned my head back on the headrest. Where was our relationship taking us? I pushed the button of my seat upright to sip the hot, orange spice tea. The pungent flavor helped to clear my head. I opened the packet of cookies and took a tiny bite off the corner of it, calming my nerves slightly as the plane sped north to Oregon. Soon, I would be home to Dominican and sort everything out.

Before returning to work, I drove to Lincoln City to meet with the lawyer, James Coburn. Eventually, he explained, the house would be transferred into my name, but for the time being, I had to wait until everything was processed by the probate judge. As I talked with Coburn, he finally glanced up from the paperwork, at last noticing my sad, reddened eyes. "Uh, Ms. McMillen, I am sorry for your loss. Dr. Jordan was truly a gentleman as well as a revered scholar. He, uh, had no heirs and no family to speak of, you understand? Therefore, he explicitly directed that all of his estate goes to you." Mr. Coburn spoke gently.

"Yes. I grew to love him as if he were my own grandfather." I reached for a tissue and loudly blew my nose. The honking sound reverberated throughout the high-ceilinged office. Self-conscious, I quickly shoved the crumpled tissue back into my purse and perched nervously on the edge of my chair. Before the session ended, the lawyer handed over a packet of paperwork, entitling me to Dr. Jordan's bank accounts, in which he had already listed me as P.O.D., his recipient upon death. When I left and scurried to my car, I plopped down into the driver's seat, and let the tears flow. It was too much, too soon. I had already lost my adopted father, Sean McMillen, to a heart attack just a few brief years before; my bio mother, Stephanie, earlier this year, and my real father had refused to acknowledge me after searching for him for two years. Before that, I had experienced the traumatizing rape incident while searching for my cold-hearted, scientist father! Now Dr. Jordan had died. I felt so alone.

Eventually, I knew I had to let Claire and Preston know the result of my latest quest to locate my missing father. They had tried so hard to help me in that endeavor. I just didn't have the energy to call them today. I would save that for when I got back into my work routine and needed to talk to someone during the lonely evenings.

After I arrived at the apartment, I hugged Dominican to my chest, while he rumbled nonstop. The vibrations of his purr were comforting. He was my cat now—Dr. Jordan was really gone. I had driven by the cemetery on my way out of Lincoln City and saw where he was buried. The fact saddened me, but at the same time, Dominican comforted me as well. Reluctantly, I decided to call Tully to let her know that I was safely home. I reached for a cup of coffee before calling. "Mom, I'm home now. I found my real father, but he refused to even talk to me." I had forgotten how satisfying it was to share with her. She always supported and encouraged me no matter what. It occurred to me that I had always taken her for granted—and she was always there for me.

"Oh, Cassie. I'm so sorry. What happened?" Tully's voice was full of empathy and love. I wept as I described my journey to the glorious butterflies, meeting up with Luis, and finally locating my father on the mountain top. Then I recounted to Tully how I had heard about Dr. Jordan's demise from the lawyer's email, and the meeting with Mr. Coburn in Lincoln City. I even explained how I would inherit Dr. Jordan's estate.

"Oh my, Cassie. Are you sure about that? What about Dr. Jordan's relatives?"

I sighed, hesitating before my reply. "No, Mom, there are no relatives. He put my name on his accounts, his will, his house—on everything. I had no idea. I just thought I was to take care of his cat, Dominican."

"Wow. That's a lot to think about."

"You have no idea, Mom. I feel so overwhelmed—and bummed out. I'm sad about Dr. Jordan and depressed about how my real father discarded me out of hand after I finally found him on top of that mountain, in the butterfly sanctuary. He hides out from the world up there, Mom. I found out that he has all his supplies delivered there, including his mail."

"Well, I suppose that's what some scientists do, Cassie. I am truly sorry. But at least, now you know."

"Right. I know now that he never wanted me either. Just like my bio mom, except that when I read her letter, written to me, I saw that she loved me at least, and tried to do the best for me."

"Yes, that should be a comfort to you. But know this, Cassie. Your dad and I loved you from the moment we saw you and brought you home into our lives."

"I'm beginning to understand that now. Thanks, Mom. Sorry I never told you before." I saved the part about Luis asking me to marry him until another day. It was all too much at once. My mind was reeling with the turn of events.

Chapter 30

I returned to the newspaper office the next day, armed with my latest feature story on the Monarchs at least half written, and some stunning photos of the butterflies on my camera. The office employees were happy to see me, and I dove into my work, cranking out a full story plausible enough to turn in for publishing. My heart wasn't in it, but I plowed through the day. I raced home to Dominican as soon as five o'clock arrived.

"Where are you hurrying out to, Cassie?" It was Jason, the sports editor. He caught up with me easily, taking long strides. He was tall and lanky; I was no match to outdistance him. I just wanted to duck into my car and speed away.

"Well, uh, I need to get home to feed my cat," I answered lamely. I wanted to exit quickly as I was in no mood to chit chat. Too many issues were lodged in the back of my brain, waiting for a chance to pour out of my subconscious and analyzed again.

"I just thought, uh, maybe you could meet me over at The Bean for a cup of coffee or something. If," he broke off, suddenly feeling inadequate when I kept my eyes down and gripped my keys, "that is, you aren't too busy or something." Jason stared at me with hazel eyes, his sandy blonde hair falling into them. For the first time, I took note that he was handsome in spite of his sometimes-awkward way. "Can your cat wait just thirty minutes or so?"

I didn't see a way out. "I suppose. See you there." I inserted my key into the door and jerked it open. So close! I almost got away without speaking to anyone.

Jason's eyes lit up as he smiled. "Great! See you in five minutes!"

I TOOK A SIP OFF THE LATTE I ORDERED WHILE JASON DRONED on, smiling and gesturing, about his latest story on the Beavers team training for their upcoming season. I smiled politely, nodding, but seeing in Jason's countenance, Luis, instead. What was he doing right now? Studying at the university, or roaming the campus with friends? I had no idea, but I missed him terribly. This guy Jason was nice, and cute too, but I realized at that very moment, that I loved Luis. I said little, but at last, Jason paused, catching his breath. "So, Cassie, how was the excursion to the Monarch sanctuary? Get a good story out of it?" His eyes bored into mine, attentive, awaiting my reply.

I snapped alert, realizing he had asked me something about the butterflies. "Uh, yeah. It was great. I'm almost finished with my story. Turning it in tomorrow." I took another swig. The latte was too sweet, already lukewarm. I set it down, hoping my answer was enough.

"That's it? Tell me more about what it was like there. I would like to go there someday." I still wore the arm sling, so I found it easy to relay how we had to ride horseback to the summit of the sanctuary, and how my horse bolted and threw me off. That seemed to pique Jason's interest, and I found myself reliving the experience once more, describing the myriads of fluttering black and orange butterflies. Thankfully, before long, Jason said he needed to go to pick up his sister, and we left the coffee shop. I didn't have to discuss the utter disappointment at finding my father. Relieved and freed at last, I drove home to Dominican, who waited for me at the front door.

THE PHONE RANG, WITH LUIS ON THE OTHER END. IT WAS almost as if he knew I had met with another man and had just arrived home. My face grew hot at the sound of his voice, and I felt guilty for meeting with Jason. As I talked with Luis, my mind rationalized the time with Jason. It was only a catch-up work meeting since I have been on assignment in Mexico, I told myself. "So, Cassie," Luis was saying, did you hear what I just said? You aren't saying much. Cassie?"

"Uh, yes. You were telling me about the latest eye surgery research. I was listening. Sure. It's just—that's more your expertise in the medical field, not mine. I pretty much gave up on surgeries to restore sight to my eye a long time ago." It sounded a little lame, but true as well. I really wasn't listening much, but also knew I didn't want to set myself up for another letdown with a failed eye operation.

"Cassie, I know you have been disappointed in the past, but this is a new breakthrough. I've been doing some reading on it, and there's a professor here that has shared some findings with me. Give it some thought, okay?"

"Uh, I don't know, Luis. I've been through that too many times. All of the so-called new research ended in failed results. No improvement in restoring sight to my eye whatsoever. I don't think I could put myself through that again. Can you understand?"

"Well, of course. But really. Just give it some thought. It's a brand-new discovery. I read about the successes of those who underwent the surgery, and there was a ninety-nine percent success rate. People could see again, Cassie. That's worth thinking about."

"Okay. I'll think about it. But I've been through a lot recently and don't really want to worry about a surgery anytime soon. There's the recovery time and all of that."

"Fair enough. I'll check back with you on it, though. I really think you will be glad if you go through with it. There's even an ophthalmologist in Portland who is familiar with the procedure." Luis sighed, and said nothing for a few seconds. I could tell he was trying to formulate what to say next. "And, uh, Cassie, the main reason I called you was to tell you that I love you. When will you agree to marry me?"

"Oh, Luis, I—I think I— love you, too," I managed to whisper. "I realized it today. I miss you, Luis."

Luis chuckled. "Just today, huh?" That's alright. It sounds wonderful that you finally said it. So, when Cassie?"

I hesitated—I felt pressure. "I don't know yet. Can you come up here to visit me soon? Maybe then we can discuss it more."

"It's difficult to get the paperwork to come to the U.S., but I'll see what I can do. Maybe on a travel or student visa. I'll check into it. You might have to return down here."

"Okay, Luis. But I think I've used up all my feature journal stories on location down there. However, maybe I can get some time off if need be." We left it at that, and I hung up, relieved to pet Dominican while watching the evening news. He purred beside me on the sofa contentedly.

I DECIDED THAT ON FRIDAY I WOULD DRIVE UP TO SPRINGVILLE to visit Mom and my sister, Jasmine. For some reason, Luis' idea of the eye surgery burrowed its way into my mind, and I found myself considering it. Perhaps, after all, I should meet with this ophthalmologist in Portland, just to get information. First, though, I wanted to run it by Mom and Jasmine. I hadn't seen them since my latest trip to Mexico anyway. As I drove, my mind wavered with the many considerations hanging in the balance. Luis had proposed marriage, but there was the uncertainty of how we could even make that work with the difference of his citizenship status and mine. There was my father's total disregard and rejection, Dr. Jordan's demise, and his house being mine eventually. Then there was the surgery. I don't have time for a surgery. What was I thinking? My cell phone startled me, alerting me as I sped along the I-5 freeway. I didn't answer it but pulled over at the nearest rest stop. It was Claire. She left a voice message. I listened to it and called her back. "Hey, girlfriend, what's going on up there? Preston and I are waiting for your report of the latest butterfly trip. Did you find your father yet? Even Tommy emailed me to ask about you."

"Well, you might as well know that I did find my father, but he refused to talk to me and shut the door in my face. Literally. End of story. On the way back down the mountainside, I fell off my horse and sprained the ligaments of my elbow. It's mending slowly."

"Oh, Cassie, I'm sorry. I had hoped that your father would welcome you with open arms. What a jerk."

"Yeah, nothing new, really. Oh, and Dr. Jordan died, and I inherited all of his stuff, including his house." I paused. "Oh, and Luis proposed to me."

"What? And you're just now telling me all of this because I called you first? When were you going to call me?" Claire was indignant, I could tell.

"I—I was going to after it all settled in my mind. Plus, Luis wants me to try a new surgery for my blind eye. It's all so overwhelming. I'm on my way to Springville to visit Mom and my sister. I just need time to sort it all out. Wanna come up to visit me? I could use a friend right now."

"I'll see what I can do. It would be great to be with you again, Cass. May I tell Preston and Tommy all of your news?"

"Yeah, I suppose. At least then I don't have to tell them myself. Thanks, Claire." We said goodbye, and I continued the drive north to Springville.

Chapter 31

"Welcome home, Cassie," Tully greeted me at her door, arms open to hug, while Sebastian and Mandy peered warily at me from around the corner of the hall.

"Hey, Mom. Feels good to be back." It really did. I didn't realize how much I needed to be here. Home. There was warmth in saying the word to myself as I flung my overnight bag onto the spare room bed. Why had I waited so long to return? My eyes watered with emotion when I knew Mom wasn't looking. I surveyed the room; it held Tully's desk where she still wrote stories for the local paper. I skimmed her latest one lying on the desk, which didn't seem quite finished yet. It featured an elderly woman who volunteered to read to students in the elementary school nearby. Sebastian sauntered in to rub up against my leg. He remembered me—I was amazed at how he never forgot, no matter how long it had been since he last saw me. Soon, Mandy ventured in, but crouched under the bed to observe me from a distance.

"Cassie, Jasmine is coming at six to join us for dinner. I thought we would have chicken and rice casserole. Is that okay for you?" Tully popped her head in the door, grinning broadly, obviously happy to have me under her roof once more.

"Uh, sure, Mom. Anything. I gave her a smile to reassure her. My confusion dissipated, leaving me strangely at peace. This was truly the medicine I needed and craved right now. Home. The rejection by my real father, the death of Dr. Jordan, uncertainty of a long-term commitment with Luis, a possible eye surgery, all evaporated into the recesses of my consciousness. All that mattered for the moment was being home with my loving, adoptive mom, my sister Jasmine, and the cats—my family.

Jasmine swooped into the house shortly before six. "Hey, Sis, what took you so long to come up here to visit? She also lugged in an overnight bag and tossed it down on the floor of the living room. "I'll claim the couch tonight, no worry." She gave me a quick hug and plopped down on a chair.

"I know you will. I already put my stuff in the spare bedroom," I retorted, laughing good naturedly.

"Sooo, what gives? You're almost a stranger here now. It's been too long."

"I know, I know. I'll tell you more at dinner. With Mom. So, how's college life?"

"Oh, same ol', same ol'. But I'm finishing up very soon! Graduating. Then I can get a job teaching music to kids. How's that for your little sis, huh?" She jabbed me in the ribs as we joined Tully in the kitchen to finish up getting the dinner ready. Mom pulled her good china out, and Jasmine and I set the table, just like the old days.

I was mentally debating what to start talking about when Mom looked over her cup at me and asked, "So, did you find your biological father this time?"

Ugh. A difficult place for me to begin, but there it was. "Well, yes. I found him on the mountain top with the butterflies. He lives there to study them." I stared at my plate, and then took a small bite of the casserole.

"And?" Mom persisted. Jasmine looked at me expectantly. Suddenly, I couldn't say more. My eyes teared up, and I wiped at them with my napkin.

"So, he kicked you off his property or something, right?" Jasmine interjected.

"Uh, yeah, pretty much," I managed to say.

Mom reached over to grab my left hand. She meant to comfort me, but I jerked my hand away. My stomach tightened into knots— I couldn't eat anymore. I jumped up and excused myself, sprinting to the spare bedroom. Sebastian was already lying there on the bed, as if sensing that I would need his comfort. I threw myself face down and sobbed, while Sebastian purred loudly at my side. I don't know what came over me—all my uncertainties and disappointments just seemed too much. I could hear Jasmine and Mom murmuring softly in the dining room, probably trying to figure out what to do. They ended up finishing their dinners quietly, and later, waited for me to return to the living room. They were drinking tea from Mom's fine china cups and watching a game show on T.V.

"Want some peppermint tea, Cassie? Your favorite?" There was an extra cup on her serving tray along with the tea pot; she didn't wait for an answer and poured me a cup. Woodenly, I accepted it after lowering gently onto the sofa. Jasmine was perched at the opposite end of the couch, but she scooched over to put her arm around my shoulders.

"You don't have to say anymore, Cass. Just know that we're here for you. Always have been."

"Thanks, Jas. Appreciate it. I just need to soak up being home with both of you, and the cats too. You know," I brightened a little, "I have a cat now, too. Dr. Jordan's cat— Dominican. He's a big grey cat, all heart. I have him plus everything else of Dr. Jordan's. He died recently, and even left me his house, which I'll get once all the legal work is done. Can you believe it?"

Both Tully and Jasmine were duly shocked, their eyes wide in surprise. The topic of Dr. Jordan opened the door to discuss at least that part of my tumultuous life right now. The rest would have to wait until later. That was all I could handle for one evening. It was just good to be home in Tully's house.

Chapter 32

"So, Mom, what do you think? Do I put myself through yet another eye surgery, even though the procedure has never been a success so far? Luis studies medicine, you know, and says there is a lot of new research on a new type of eye surgery to restore sight." I paused long enough to take a sip off the coffee Tully had just made. She poured herself a cup, giving herself a moment before answering me.

"Well, Cassie, it seems to me that you are an adult woman who can make that decision intelligently. How do you feel about it?" Tully walked over to the table and sat down with her coffee. I followed suit. Before I could sit down onto the chair, she added, "and just who is this Luis? Your boyfriend? You haven't told me much, other than you met him in Mexico, and then he met up with you at the butterfly sanctuary. Hmm?" She looked over with a playful grin.

"Well, yes, you could call him my boyfriend. And I met his whole family when I went to Puebla on assignment. They are a very nice family. And, uh, by the way, I guess you could say he is also my finance." I laughed nervously, hoping to cover my embarrassment. "Nothing official. I haven't even really said yes—for sure. Still processing it all."

"He's what? Why didn't you say so to begin with? Cassie?" Tully raised her voice a bit, more than she had intended, but it was all so unexpected. "When? The wedding, I mean."

I got up to refill my coffee cup in order to give me a few seconds before my reply. "Well, Mom, I don't know yet. He and I need to get together first to figure it all out. I'm still kind of overwhelmed at the idea as well. I need some time to sort it all out, what with my bio father's rejection, Dr. Jordan's passing, and now this surgery idea. So much to consider all at once, you know?"

"Sure, Sweetie, I get that. Don't rush to make a decision about either a wedding or a surgery. I'm just happy you paid us a visit to catch up."

"Yeah, I wasn't sure how to tell you everything on the phone. I needed to drive up to tell you both in person. Maybe you can help me tell Jas. She'll give me a hard time. Guess she's sleeping in."

"Tell me what?" Jasmine stumbled into the kitchen, heading straight for the coffee pot. Her strawberry blonde hair poked out at odd angles, a tangled mane.

"Uh, give me a minute. Drink some coffee first and I'll run it all by you." My mind was scattered, trying to decide where to start. Mom just smiled encouragingly. She would help me.

THE WEEKEND ENDED ALL TOO QUICKLY, AND I WAS BACK IN the newspaper office early Monday morning. It was a good thing that Claire was flying up to visit me for the upcoming weekend. She would help me sort out my decisions, or at least, she was always a good listener. I looked forward to seeing her. The crushing blow of finding my father, who rudely refused me, still niggled at my emotions. Claire would help me rise above my injured feelings.

As Monday wore on at the office, I couldn't help but observe how Jason kept giving me the eye and smiling over his computer. I just wanted to slip out unnoticed and unaccompanied when the end of the workday drew near. It wasn't to be. As I marched out the door, Jason jumped up from his desk and followed me out like a puppy dog. "Hey, Cassie, wanna get another cup of joe someplace?" I didn't break stride—just kept walking. Darn. I had almost made it out the door. "Or, how about going to that new pub over on First Street for a brewsky? Which sounds better to you?"

I had to acknowledge at this point. "Well, uh, Jason, I'm expecting my friend from California to call after work. Gotta run." Lame excuse. I didn't know if Claire would call or not. But she might. After all, she was flying up this weekend. I could call her to make my statement sort of true.

"Okay. But how about tomorrow after work? You choose where." He held the door open for me and I slipped through, eager to be outside. There was no getting out of this one nimbly.

"All right, Jason. Let's try the new place on First Street. I'll be ready for a drink by tomorrow. Unless something else comes up?" I had to have an escape route just in case.

"Sure. Tomorrow then." He smiled so sweetly, and I felt a rush of something. He was so good looking in his sandy blonde way. I finally reached my car and unlocked the door. He grinned as he swung it open with his left hand, gesturing with his right, the genteel gentleman. I slid into the driver's seat and looked up. He bent down and smiled at me, too close to my face for comfort. I turned on the ignition to signal that I desired to go. He relinquished the door and shut it softly. "Bye, Cass. See you tomorrow!"

"Bye," I said from inside the car, and put it into reverse. Really, I thought. I'm not leading him on. What's the deal? I had never, in all my days, been pursued by a man, and now two? Well, there was that one—the guy who raped me. But he didn't count at all. What was happening? I needed to chat with Claire. I was so glad she was going to visit this weekend. She would help sort it all out. She had much more experience at men than I did.

Tuesday after work I kept my promise to Jason and met him at the First Street Pub. I tried not to smile any more often than I had to, attempting to discourage him from thinking there was any interest. He seemed oblivious. He just rattled on about his latest sports article, the one featuring the Oregon State basketball team, and their chances of going to finals. I managed to nod politely, and take a sip off my drink, and then mumble "Um hmm" now and then. My mind was far away, up with the butterflies on the mountaintop in Mexico.

"So, what do you think, Cassie?" Jason stared at me expectantly, awaiting an answer to something.

Uh oh. He caught me daydreaming. "Uh, ask me again? I'm sorry," I sputtered, my face getting hot with guilt. He was such a nice guy after all. And handsome. *Why was I treating him so badly? Was I really that heartless? How would I feel if he were me?"*

"What's the deal, Cassie? I was just asking your professional opinion if I should call the O.S.U. coach for an interview or just show up at their next game? Are you okay, Cassie? You seem distracted about something." Jason took a swig off his beer, and set it down a bit loudly, but waited for me to answer something. What do I say?"

"Well, I, uh, do have things on my mind. One thing is, uh, my best friend is flying up this weekend from California and I have to get everything ready. You know, for her visit and all. I have to have my articles ready before she arrives, you know." Wow. Was that ever a weak excuse. I just couldn't go into my surgery dilemma or Dr. Jordan, or least of all, Luis. What else could I say? I hoped it was enough.

"Sure, sure. But what do you think I should do? Call the coach or not?" Jason persisted. My excuse seemed to satisfy him, but he still asked for my viewpoint. I drained my glass first, searching mentally for the best answer. After all, he did ask my professional opinion.

"Well, Jason, it's always a good idea to go to the source first. In this case, it's the coach. Try to get the interview before their next game. If he declines to meet with you, then grab what you can on the fly at the game. Maybe go into the locker room, and talk to guys on the team, and maybe the coach too, if he's in there. You have an advantage, in this case, being male. You can enter their domain. I wouldn't be able to do that unless I was covering the women's team." I chuckled at my own joke. He laughed, too.

"Good idea, Cass. I knew you would have the best approach. I've read your stories. They are excellent—especially your interviews one-on-one." The compliment was genuine, and it made me smile. He really was such a nice guy.

Chapter 33

"So, what do you think, Claire?" I breathed deeply, pausing as I related all my worries, including Luis' proposal as well as Jason and his friend wanting to meet with Claire and me this evening at the First Street Pub. She and I were sitting on my apartment patio in plastic chairs, sipping our morning coffee.

"Well, Cass, first of all, you and Luis are not formally engaged, right? Plus, you have never slept with him, right? I nodded meekly. "So, what's the deal? Let's go out with Jason and his friend tonight and enjoy ourselves. We can figure out the rest of your decisions as we go. Plus, have you gone shopping lately? I need a new outfit. Claire's eyes flashed brightly at the thought of going out that evening and having a reason to go shopping.

"But—but I must make it clear to Jason that this is only a friendship date, not a real one. He keeps asking me to meet him someplace after work. I do have a boyfriend, you know," I sniffed defensively.

"Yeah, yeah, do that all later. I'm here, the men will be at the pub, it's all good. Let's get some stylin' clothes to wear. You probably need some. I've seen what you wear."

"Well, thanks a lot, Claire. My clothes aren't that bad." I feigned umbrage. In a mock huff, I got up with my coffee cup and went into the kitchen.

"True, but we want to feel like we are knocking these guys out when we enter, you know? Good for the ol' self-esteem. May even help you with all the decisions you are making. Who knows?"

Claire grinned, following me into the house. We had a quick breakfast of cold cereal and dressed for our shopping trip.

It was all so Deja vu—just like the first time when I met the guy who assaulted me on the island. But now, I was much the wiser, much more experienced with the dating scene. None-the-less, we made a similar entrance into the pub. Claire led the way, with her signature red spikey hair, standing up on its glorious end, her svelte hips, swaying in her new bright red stilettos. She purchased black skinny jeans and a white light-weight sweater, covered in bling. She looked stunning. Men sitting at the bar visibly turned to stare appreciatively, taking her all in. Claire loved entrances, that's all I've got to say. I trailed behind her, in my new outfit of navy capris with a canary yellow shell. I had also bought perky yellow flats. I never felt comfortable in heels, so why not? My jet-black Afro, now nearly touching my shoulders, was noticeable in the eatery. I didn't see anyone else with one. But then, who else had spikey red hair? We were quite the scene. I gave Claire a nudge, so she would know which direction to strut toward. I saw Jason and his friend in the back at a tall table with two extra stools. Jason's friend, Andrew, nearly popped his eyes out of their sockets as we approached, although he immediately glanced down at his glass. He wore dark rimmed glasses and was dressed in khakis and a blue button-down shirt. Jason was similarly dressed, like the uniform of a stodgy professor or something.

Jason hopped up from his stool to greet us, stammering and nervous, practically knocking it over. Claire had a way of making that happen with men. I had to look down to keep from laughing. "So, Claire, this is my coworker, Jason, and his friend." Formally,

Jason stuck out his hand for a shake, and mumbled, gesturing with his free hand to Andrew.

"Uh, Andrew, Claire, and uh, Cassie." Everyone shook hands and then we sat down on the stools to order drinks. Conversation was mundane, sketchy. Claire and I found out that Andrew worked for a marketing agency, which made for a few minutes of banter. Claire also volunteered that she lived and worked in the L.A. area for a designer clothing outfit. That, too, sparked some talk, and then we veered to Jason's and my newspaper, and the various articles we had written recently. When Claire jumped up to go to the ladies' room, I looked down at my drink to make sure it was empty—the memory of the sordid evening still raw and fresh, even after all this time. I excused myself and walked in Claire's wake, the sea of men parting as she swaggered to the back of the pub.

"So, Claire, what do you think? I caught my breath, waiting for her approval or not. We stood near the sinks of the restroom, Claire preening and touching up her hair in the mirror as we spoke softly. She applied more of her scarlet red lipstick.

"Sure, sure, great for the night's outing. Thanks for setting it up, Cass. I hope that Luis is a bit more dashing than these two. Nice career types, though."

I felt my face redden. "Yeah, of course he is. Luis is pretty cool, being the Latin type and all. Dark and handsome, medical student, nice family. You'll have to meet him."

"Oh, really? And tall too or just dark and handsome?" Claire teased, grinning at me in the mirror as she applied yet another coating of bright red lipstick.

"Well, to be honest, about my height. I'm sort of tall for a girl." I was still dead serious, wondering where this was leading to. I opened my purse and pulled out my trusty tube of shell pink lipstick, applying some to keep up with Claire. I smacked my lips together—the sound echoing in the high-ceilinged restroom.

"Okay. That's good enough. A doctor. I like that part too. And Cass, you need to get him to put a ring on your finger while he's still in the mood, you know? He sounds like a catch."

"Really? It's just all so much, and so fast."

"The good things in life always seem to come that way, girlfriend. Now let's go back out there and enjoy our evening with these guys."

I gasped and stared at her in the mirror.

"Not that way, silly. Just a pleasant night out at the pub. Okay?"

"Sure, Claire. Whatever."

Chapter 34

The weekend with Claire flew by in a rush, with us chatting late into the nights about numerous topics, including my pending decisions. All too soon, it was time for her flight home to Los Angeles. After she left, I was still confused about getting married to Luis, but I allowed myself to consider the eye surgery. Claire encouraged me, saying, "At least, give it one more attempt. You still have your whole life ahead of you." I reserved a small corner of my conscience to change my mind.

Luis and I still wanted to meet in person to discuss our future possibility together either here or in in Mexico. We would have to figure out a date for that. In the meantime, I resolved to call the ophthalmologist in Portland for a conference appointment to weigh the advantages of an eye surgery. After all, I could always decline the surgery once I found out the details. What to do with my eventual beach home from Dr. Jordan would have to wait, but I daydreamed about a future at the coast with Luis. Maybe it would work out one day to be married…I just didn't know yet.

On Monday, I focused on work, following up on two phoned in feature story leads. One involved a veteran from World War II who still worked in the town as a part time plumber. I called him and set up the interview for the next day. The other lead was a farmer who raised llamas as therapy animals. I knew I would enjoy that story, since I loved animals. I arranged to meet him Friday on location at his farm.

As I sat concentrating on an article I was reworking, Jason sauntered by. "Hey, Cassie, Andrew and I really enjoyed our get together Friday with you and Claire." He grinned, giving me a jab on my elbow. "Know what I mean? Can we do that again?"

"Well, as you know, Claire lives in L.A. and returned there last evening. I don't think we'll be able to do that again anytime soon." I kept typing, hoping he would get the message that I was busy and return to his own workstation and leave me alone. I didn't need his distraction right now, either for my writing or for my relationship with Luis.

"Well, granted that. She mentioned that she lived in Los Angeles. I just thought, that, er, maybe you and I could meet up again after work sometime this week—today, or later, say, tomorrow?" He stood close to my desk, a bit pathetic as he stood there, a longing expression on his face. How to let him down? I was so new at this.

"Well, uh, to be honest, I have a boyfriend. He lives out of the area, you know?" I tried to give Jason my full attention; after all, he was only being interested. Plus, he was a nice guy, and cute.

"Oh, I didn't realize that. But how about if we just extend our workday a bit at the pub—you know—talk about our stories, get suggestions from each other. Maybe we could even run our stories by one another like editors, you know?"

"I don't know—you understand it would only be for work, right?"

"Sure. I get it. Are you free today after work?" His face glowed at the thought. He really was so good looking. I was amazed that he wasn't someone's boyfriend already.

WE KEPT OUR PUB GET TOGETHER STRICTLY BUSINESS—OR AT least, I did. We read one another's current stories and offered revision suggestions for clarity. It really did help to have someone look over my work before I turned it over to the editor. Still, I felt like I was leading Jason on. To relieve the guilt, I called Luis as soon as I got home while Dominican sat on my lap. We planned our next time together, but I needed to ask my boss for time off, unless Luis could arrange the paperwork to leave Mexico and fly up. So, we had nothing to go on yet. I would wait until he checked the possibility into his travel up here. It wasn't easy, what with Mexican nationals not being allowed in the U.S. without proper credentials.

Then, out of the blue, my boss asked when I could leave for Mexico again to cover a sequel story about the Cholula Pyramid. She said that she had received many inquiries and positive feedback. She was certain there was more I could cover regarding the latest in excavation discoveries. I jumped at the chance to return—I could visit Luis and his family. I called him late that evening; I knew he was studying at Monterey, so I needed to be sure of when he could join me at Puebla.

"What a surprise, Cassie. My paperwork has been delayed for leaving Mexico to the U.S., so I'm glad you can visit here. I'm sure I can get away from Monterey whenever you want. Right now, I'm just doing extra research for my cohort." Luis sounded so happy, so reassuring.

"Okay, I'll tell my boss I'll leave here in two weeks and stay for a week there. I don't want to be gone too long this time."

"Certainly. I'll let my family know our plans. They will be thrilled to see you again."

After we hung up, I breathed deeply, remembering Luis and how much I cared for him. It will be a good excuse not to meet up with Jason after work anymore this week or next.

Chapter 35

As I deboarded the plane in Mexico City, I went over in my mind what I would say to Luis. Outside the terminal, there he was, awaiting my arrival. "Cassie. I missed you," he said, grabbing my bag and giving me a huge bearhug.

I stood there stiffly, arms at my side, speechless. I don't know why; I just didn't know what to say. "Hi, Luis. Good to see you," I finally managed to mumble before the crowds pushed us along. We took the bus to Puebla and sat together, not saying a whole lot. Why am I here? Besides covering a follow up story for my newspaper. Do I really want to get married to this guy? I don't really know him all that well. I looked out the window at the passing landscape. Luis shifted in his seat uneasily, as if expecting me to say more.

"Uh, Cassie, it's good that you're here. We have a lot to discuss." He grabbed my hand, but I kept it limp. "Is anything wrong?" His eyes bored into mine.

"Well, uh, I guess I just feel kind of overwhelmed. So much has happened in a short time, and I don't want to rush into anything, you know?"

"Oh, of course," he agreed, although I could tell that wasn't the answer he was hoping for. "We don't have to rush into anything—just talk, okay?" He changed the subject, launching into a long litany of his latest studies at the university. He mentioned casually that he would finish and be ready to go into practice by June of this year. Numbly, I nodded, wondering just what that could mean. I didn't realize until that moment that he was finishing so soon. I continued to watch the hills and sparce grass flit by the window. I needed some space to think and looked forward to getting a hotel with a room to myself near the pyramid. My employer would pay, of course.

As it turned out, the hotel was the same one I had stayed in the first time in Cholula. The old downtown area afforded only a few options, and I needed to set up base there for easy access. Luis and I said goodbye from there, with the agreement that I would join him in Puebla when my assignment was finished. When I reached the small hotel room, I threw my bag on the floor, heaved myself onto the bed, and took a fitful nap. The trip had been fatiguing and long. I just wanted to forget about Luis for the moment— forget the trauma on the island, forget the crushing rejection from my real father, my impending eye surgery, and all the legal matters pertaining to Dr. Jordan. Here I was, back where I ended my search in Mexico. What had I really gained through it all?

I awoke two hours later, hungry, and disoriented. I looked around at the sparce furnishings of the hotel room: a small bed covered by a worn quilt, a nightstand, a wooden chair and writing table, and a closet. There was no T.V. and no bathroom. Again, I had to share a bathroom at the end of the hall. I stumbled out of my room to use the toilet and throw water on my face. I had to get control of my emotions; after all, I had an assignment to turn in for my editor from Cholula. This time, I would attempt to cover the town itself, and perhaps, if they cooperated with me, talk to a few of the locals. I wasn't sure how that would go. If not, my story would focus on food and customs, and photos of the picturesque village. Grabbing my camera, notebook, and backpack, I staggered down the steps of the hotel and onto the bustling street of Cholula.

Four days later, I arrived by bus in Puebla to meet up with Luis and his family. Three days remained before I had to return back to the States. I had my story, at least, the rough draft of one, and many pictures to go with it. I hoped that my editor would be satisfied. Now for the hard part—Luis and his family. I took a deep breath and got off the bus in the Puebla bus depot. There he was, all smiles, arms ready to embrace me. "Welcome home, Cassie."

Breaking from his embrace, I looked up into his face. "What are you talking about, Luis?" I felt embarrassed—so off balance. I shook him off, pretending I needed to adjust my backpack.

"Nothing—just that my family and I feel you are part of our family already. We love you, Cassie. That's all."

"Okay, well, don't do that. Not yet. We haven't even talked yet." I grabbed my extra bag, refusing his attempt to take it for me. I hated myself—I was off to a wrong start before we even got out of the depot. I just didn't want to feel rushed or pressured. I had to take this gradually, I realized now. Luis practically ran to keep up with me as we made our way to the taxi pickup area.

After we go into the cab and were zipping along the busy city streets, I let out a sigh, formulating the words to say in my mind first. "Uh, Luis, uh, I have decided that I want to get a room somewhere, and not stay with your family this time. Is that okay with you?"

"What do you mean? Stay in a hotel here, in Puebla?"

"Yes. That's what I mean. I just need a little space, Luis. Your family is great and all, but I know I will feel stifled—pressured. We have to talk first, remember?" I looked up into his face; he appeared confused, and a bit hurt. "Please, Luis?" I took his hand in mine, hoping to soften the request.

"Well, uh, Cassie, my mom set up a room for you, and has all these meals planned. She will be extremely disappointed. As will I," he finished, looking down at our hands. "What will I tell my family?" He was at a loss, not knowing how to interpret this request.

"Will it help to tell them that my employer is paying for my hotel? They actually are, in fact. I just need to find one that isn't too expensive. I can come for the dinners your mother planned, and visit, right?" I attempted to seem hopeful, positive. "I just want to feel free to talk with only you first, and then work my way to your family. I have so much to deal with right now. Can you possibly understand, Luis?"

"I guess so," he answered morosely. "Let me redirect the taxi driver to a hotel near our neighborhood."

Soon we were at the curb of a hotel, and the driver handed over my bag. Luis grabbed it before I could, and we walked up the steps of the hotel together. I checked in, got my key, and Luis accompanied me to the door of the room. "I'll meet you in the lobby in ten minutes. Just let me get settled a bit."

"Sure, I'll be there waiting." He tried to smile, but it appeared forced. I closed the door, and sat down on the bed, trying to compose myself. What had come over me? I felt close to panic at the mere sight of him and prospect of going to stay at his parents'. Why?

Chapter 36

I entered the lobby fifteen minutes later. I could see Luis pacing the floor, looking at his watch. He heard my footsteps, glancing up and grinning, clearly relieved that I arrived. He approached, grabbing both of my hands. "Want to get something to drink at the bar here? My mother is preparing dinner for us tonight, but at least we can sit and have a beverage."

"Sure. Maybe they have a club soda or something bubbly. That would be good. My stomach is a bit edgy after the bus ride." Luis touched my back gently, steering me towards the lounge area of the hotel. We entered and found a secluded table near a corner in the back. I sat down across from Luis, who immediately took both my hands in his, and stared into my eyes. A server stopped by, and I ordered the club soda, and Luis ordered a Corona.

Within seconds, it seemed, our drinks were served on the table. I took a long sip, the bubbly action of the club soda sizzling all the way down my throat. "So, are you playing hard to get today? My mother made up my sister's room for you, but here you are, in this starchy hotel." He gazed around at the walls, as if emphasizing his point. He attempted levity and humor, but it wasn't working for me.

"Oh, Luis. I don't know what's wrong with me. I'm just panicked and scared. What does it mean?"

"What has happened with you to feel that way, Cassie? I think I have always treated you gently, and taken everything slow, right? Did I do something to hurt you or offend you? What's going on?"

Softly, he rubbed my hands inside his, and looked steadily at me. "You can tell me anything, really. It's okay."

"Uh, not now. Maybe later, after I have been here for a couple of days. Can we just forget it for now and try to enjoy being together, and with your family?" I felt trapped—I just couldn't talk about whatever it was that was troubling me at the moment. I wasn't even certain what it was that made me feel agitated. I hoped I would know eventually. It was already too much just to be here. Maybe I would loosen up after a day or so.

"Okay, Cass. Whatever you wish. I'm here for you, and if you need to stay in a hotel, we are fine with that. My mother gets that your boss is paying. It's a nice perk, right?" He smiled brightly, trying to lighten my mood.

"Yes, it is—thanks, Luis. Thanks for understanding." I wasn't sure why I felt the need for space in the hotel instead of with his family, but there it was. I would think about it later, by myself.

As Luis and I entered his home around five o'clock, the pungent aroma of simmering beef and spices greeted us. My stomach rumbled in protest; I didn't realize that I was so hungry until now. I still felt a bit queasy, but the dinner smelled irresistibly delicious. Maria stepped away from the kitchen to greet us with hugs and a peck on the cheek. Stiffly, I endured the hug, my arms straight down by my side. "Welcome, Cassie. Make yourself at home." Her warm smile was contagious; suddenly, I was happy to be here. My stomach relaxed—my mind felt at peace. Viviana and Mercedes also appeared in the living room, and each in turn, greeted me with a hug and kiss on the cheek. Still, I kept my arms down, but the gesture from them was genuine.

"Esteban will be here soon," Maria called out from the kitchen. This was exactly how I remembered coming here the first time. It was good to be back; suddenly, I felt a twinge of guilt that I had booked the hotel room instead of staying here. I wondered how to broach the topic, since Luis said his mother had been planning for me to stay there.

Fortunately, I didn't have to say anything. Luis took care of it. "Mom, Cassie told me that her employer is paying for her hotel room, so she won't be staying here."

Maria's head appeared around the corner from the kitchen. Her eyebrows were knitted together in confusion. "What did you say? She's not staying here? I already made-up Vivian's room for her." She sounded disappointed.

"I know, Mom, but how can she refuse her boss?" He looked back at her cheerily, trying to convey that all was well.

"Well, all right then. You must see her to her hotel each evening. We need to make sure she is safe." Maria's motherly tone left no room for argument.

"Of course, Mom. I intend to do just that," he added, staring at me pointedly to let me know there would be no argument with me as well. I looked down, feeling a bit foolish, but was grateful, realizing they all wanted to keep me safe.

After Luis' father, Esteban arrived, we gathered at the dining table to eat. Vivian and Mercedes helped Maria with serving the succulent shredded beef, served with tortillas and vegetables. "So, Cassie, Luis tells me that you are here on another journal assignment," Esteban stated, directing the conversation my way.

"Yes, Mr. Mendez. My newspaper editor wants me to do a follow up on the culture, architecture, and people of Cholula, to kind of go with my other story on the pyramid itself. I covered that one last time I was here, if you remember." I felt put on the spot but tried to carry on a decent conversation.

"Yes, that's right. I remember. And you may call me Esteban if you wish. I don't need the formality," he chuckled, diving into another bite of beef, followed by a tortilla. Luis gave me a grateful glance, indicating that I was doing fine. Dinner talk continued, but I was glad when Luis steered the topic away from me, and talked about his latest research at the university, plus his near completion of medical school. My stomach relaxed a bit when the focus was off me, and I was able to eat a portion of the scrumptious meal. Soon, we convened in the living room for lime sorbet, served in small glass dessert bowls. Mercedes offered coffee as well, as we were seated for more small talk.

I was relieved when dinner was over, and I could return to the hotel for some me time. Luis escorted me there, of course, and at the door to my room, gave me a quick kiss on the lips. "You did great with my family, Cassie. I'll see you tomorrow."

"Thank you, Luis. I tried really hard, but I am exhausted now. Being by myself here will be just what I need. Don't be early. I'll take breakfast in the hotel and work awhile on my story if it's okay with you. Maybe we could meet after lunch?"

"Uh, sure, if that's what you want. You only have a couple of days here, though, and I was hoping to spend some quality time with you." He looked crestfallen; I felt guilty.

"Well, maybe we could get a late lunch together, then, say, one o'clock. Pick me up here?"

"Yes—yes, of course. See you then."

After I closed the door, I remained with my back hugging the door; only then did I allow the tears to fall. What had come over me since I arrived in Puebla? I collapsed onto the bed and cried myself to sleep, and stayed there, fully clothed until morning.

I awoke at six and ordered breakfast in my room. I showered and then dove into my article for a couple of hours. Before I realized it, it was time to meet Luis for lunch. He knocked softly on my door, precisely at one. My heart skipped a beat, and I opened it, to see Luis holding a lovely pink bouquet of roses. "For you—my love." I held the door ajar, not sure if I wanted him to come in. "May I come in?" He didn't wait for an answer but stepped inside. He set the flowers, already in a vase, on the small table next to my laptop. I still had said nothing. "How are you today? Get some sleep?"

"Uh, yes. I'm better, I think. I fell asleep as soon as you dropped me off last evening." That wasn't exactly true, but I did lie down right away. I glanced over at the roses. "Thanks, Luis. They're beautiful."

"Yes, well, I wanted something to remind you of me when I'm not here." He grinned mischievously. "But I hope that will change for the better soon. Let's start out by having lunch, and see where that goes, okay?"

Chapter 37

Luis and I decided on lunch in the hotel dining room, where I ate a Caesar salad. It was light—no spice—and easy on my still queasy digestion. Soon, we were on the busy streets of Puebla, hand in hand, just touring around. We ended up going inside the towering cathedral, our footsteps echoing as we made our way down the aisle. We sat down on a hard wooden pew, and I looked up to the arched dome, in awe at the vastness of the cathedral. The ornate artwork was amazing; I had never seen anything like it in the U.S. The cathedral dated back to the Spanish conquistadors of the sixteenth century. Not much had changed inside or out since its original construction. Statues of angels and saints peered down at us solemnly from the bulwarks as we knelt. It was both eerie and comforting to me, a newbie to all of this. My mother, Tully, had taken Jasmine and me to mass on occasion, but the church in Springville was miniscule, new, and plain by comparison. Luis informed me that the Puebla cathedral had been patterned after the one in Mexico City, which also dated back to the Spanish conquest. Both cities were Spanish colonies, replete with churches on almost every corner. Luis mentioned that there were some two hundred in Puebla alone, and legend proclaimed that there were 365 churches in San Pedro, Cholula, one for every day of the year. In Puebla, this cathedral was the largest place of worship. Daily mass services were conducted throughout the day, several times a day, in every church location. I was awestruck by this—the open devotion to faith—so lacking in most areas of the U.S.

Reverently, Luis knelt, bowed his head, closed his eyes, and folded his hands together in prayer. I watched, and copied him, not sure what to pray, but sensing the serenity in the holy place. The sanctuary was totally silent, save an occasional footstep echoing on the marble floor, as another worshiper entered to pray. Minutes ticked by, and still Luis prayed. When he finally looked up after fifteen minutes or so, he whispered, "There is a mass starting in five minutes. Is it alright with you if we stay?"

"Uh—sure, Luis. Let's just stay then. About how long does the mass last?"

"Oh, the daily mass is about twenty to thirty minutes. Not long." He grinned at me; obviously glad I had consented to stay. We arose from the kneeling bench and slid onto the hard seat. More people quietly filed in and filled up the pews towards the front of the sanctuary. Soon, the mass began; the organ swelled with liturgical melody. The priest and a few others proceeded down the main aisle and continued to the front. Everyone seemed focused as they listened, voices singing to the cantor's music, and kneeling and praying at the proper moments. I just followed Luis' lead. The rhythm of it was soothing and serene— calming. My anxiety faded into it all, and I found myself empty of worry, at least during these moments of time.

Years ago, as a child, I had been baptized in the Church, and I remembered receiving my first communion. Now, when the time came in the mass to go forward to receive the Eucharist, I nodded to Luis that I would go with him. He looked at me questioningly, but I assured him in a nod that it was okay. We approached the priest single file, with me going first, and Luis following me. Somehow, this felt right; we were truly a couple. Perhaps we were meant to be after all. At that moment, my fears dissipated. I was never before so sure of anything in my life.

AFTER WE LEFT THE CATHEDRAL, WE STOPPED AT AN ITALIAN coffee shop, both of us aware of the euphoric moment, wishing it to continue. Unexpectedly, as we gazed into one another's eyes over our lattes, and held hands across the table, I knew my world was right. We said no words, but none were necessary. Luis bent across the small table and tenderly kissed me; both of us sensing the wondrous change. Now we could talk about our future together; nothing else mattered now. I felt certain that he was the one for me.

AS WE STROLLED DOWN THE SIDEWALK FROM THE COFFEE SHOP, hand in hand, we aimlessly entered a park, and sat down on a bench. I knew that I had to share more with him about my traumatic incident but didn't know how to broach the subject. I hated to spoil the moment, so instead, just enjoyed the closeness with him. It would have to discussed later, I decided. "So, Cassie, you have only until tomorrow to spend here in Puebla. What shall we do between now and then? Are you ready to plan a wedding or is it still too soon? Is something holding you back?"

I shrank from his touch at that question, scooting away from him on the bench. Birds called overhead from the trees nearby, and I tried to focus on the sound, and not what was bothering me. "I uh, don't know, Luis. Or don't want to say just yet."

"Why, Cassie? Is it me or what? I really need to know in order to correct something." He looked hurt— confused. Luis reached out to take my hand, but I pulled away.

"Luis, I don't want to ruin the moment. Can we speak of this later? I—I don't think I can discuss it now. It has nothing to do with you. Honest. Could we just enjoy our last day and a half together?

At least, we know we want to be married, if not exactly when yet."

Luis took a long breath, hesitating before speaking again. "Well, I need some sort of reassurance, Cass. Please. You'll be leaving soon. My parents also need something to go on." He turned to stare deeply into my face. His love shone in his expression, but also confusion. "I've respected you as a woman, and never done anything you felt uncomfortable with. What is going on?"

"Okay, Luis," I said, not wanting to go on, but realizing he needed some sort of answer. "Let's set a date a year from now. Is that good?" I was attempting to avoid the growing panic in my mind. I didn't know how to overcome it except to procrastinate.

"Yes, we can do that. But my medical training is completed, and I need to decide where to set up my practice. We need to do some serious planning. What is really going on with you?"

"Okay. Here it is. When I went to the island in Texas, before I met you, I met a guy. First date and all." It—-I put my head in my hands. "I had barely dated anyone at all before that. I didn't know much about dating—or anything." I started weeping. I couldn't go on.

"Oh, Cassie. I'm so sorry. It's okay." Luis rubbed my back, trying to comfort me. "You can share more if you want, but later, okay?"

I looked up then, my eyes swollen with tears. "Okay, Luis. Later please."

Chapter 38

Luis sensed that I needed to reflect and talk more, so he called his parents to say that we weren't going to make it for dinner. We continued our tour around the city, stopping to eat at a Chinese restaurant. I was ready to share more with him. It was as if the mass service had shattered the barrier to my heartaches. I didn't know how else to explain it. I felt free—exhilarated and liberated. The Chinese eatery was quiet; no music, just a server here and there, bringing food to tables with waiting patrons. I drew a deep breath, and plunged in. "So, Luis, before we set a date to be married and all, there is something you need to know about me, and my past." I looked down into my lap, afraid to continue.

"What is it, Cassie?" He spoke softly. "I know that you were adopted, that you have been trying to discover your identity by finding your real father, and that you recently lost a dear friend, Dr. Jordan." He took my hands in his as we sat next to one another in a booth. "What else is there, Cassie? You can tell me. I love you no matter what." I raised my head and noticed that he was searching my face with his dark eyes. He smiled encouragingly. "Remember, I am a doctor now. I was trained to be empathetic." He tried to get me to laugh, but it wasn't working yet. "No worries. What would you like to tell me?"

"I—uh—it's very difficult for me to say." I focused on my cup of tea, refilling it from the pot on the table, and refused to meet Luis' eyes. Tears fell onto my lap; both of us were silent.

Finally, Luis gently touched my shoulder. "You know, whatever happened to you is in the past. It won't matter to us. We will start a new life together."

"Luis, it will matter; I know it will. I—I'm afraid of.... you know..." I shrugged, my mouth grimacing, "the—the intimate part of marriage. I, uh, something happened to me. Something terrible. Like I was telling you, it happened on the island while I was searching for my father. It was on that first date with the guy I met there. He, uh, put something in my drink." I started weeping, and other people in the restaurant began glancing our direction. "I'm so sorry, Luis. You deserve more than this."

Luis signaled the waiter to bring our check, and hurriedly, we got up and left. Once on the street again, I calmed down. The walking helped bring me back under control of my emotions. "Okay, Cassie, I think I understand. You don't have to go into detail. You probably have PTSD, which would be normal under the circumstances. I think that perhaps, if you see a counselor for a while, it will help. Plus, now that I know, I will help you, too. We can do this together. I know we can. We will just take things slow, as we have been all along, right?" He grinned at me affectionately, grabbing my hand and swinging it as we ambled down the sidewalk.

"Okay, I think." I sniffled loudly, and Luis pulled a tissue from his pocket to give me. I felt better having him as a support. We would get through this together, instead of me trying to face my fears alone in the dark of night.

All too soon, my time in Puebla was over. I hugged his family goodbye, and he rode with me on the bus to the airport in Mexico City. Within about eight hours I was back home, and Dominican was waiting at the door to greet me. He didn't let me out of his sight, padding behind me wherever I walked inside the apartment. He jumped on my lap as I sat down, purring loudly. It was good to be home.

Chapter 39

Jasmine had finished her degree in June and was getting married to her fiancée, John, from her education class cohort. They both completed their credentials to be teachers and applied for positions in the Springville area. It was to be a July wedding, and she asked me to be her maid of honor. The wedding was to be held in Springville, so I drove up and stayed over at Tully's. The timing was perfect for me to see a church wedding up close and process the idea for my own ceremony.

Jasmine looked radiant in her ivory silk, bare-backed gown. Her strawberry blonde hair was swept up on the sides, flowing underneath her veil and onto her light porcelain skin in the back. She had chosen a peach bridesmaid dress with puffy sleeves for me to wear. My dark complexion and hair complemented the color of the dress, providing a striking contrast to her, my sweet, adopted sister and now bride. The handsome groom, John, in a black tux, stood straight at the front of the sanctuary, his eyes searching to locate Jasmine when she appeared in the processional down the aisle on the arm of our Uncle Luke. John had dark hair and eyes and was nearly as tall as Luke. Uncle Luke, as per usual, wore his hair pulled back in his silver-grey ponytail, but he looked smart in his black tux as well, grinning proudly as he escorted Jasmine to the forefront of the church. Candles and peach-colored bouquets of flowers adorned the platform as we approached.

When the couple said their vows, I had to dab at my eyes. It touched me to see my baby sister professing the solemn words. The couple seemed so sure of themselves; so in love with one another. Would I ever feel that strongly about marriage with Luis? I didn't have time to ponder the thought. At that moment, Jasmine and John were pronounced man and wife, and then they kissed. The newly married couple proceeded back down the aisle, accompanied by a recessional, as Uncle Luke and I followed. He grinned and arched his eyebrows as he took my arm, as if to say I should be next. I supposed I would be.

The reception took place in the church hall, resplendent with more peach flowers adorning each table and around the cake. I observed Jasmine and her husband giving one another the traditional bite of cake which ended up all over John's face. People laughed good naturedly. Uncle Luke offered a toast to the bride and groom, and we all sipped on champagne. All too soon, it was time for Jasmine and John to depart for their honeymoon on the Oregon coast. As she left, Jasmine threw her bouquet, and Luke yelled, "Cassie, go catch it!" I did. Everyone cheered. The older sister, me, was next, according to the tradition of bouquet catching. I wanted it to be true and hoped I would be adequate for Luis.

PART 3
Oregon

Chapter 40

The eye surgery went off smoothly; it was an outpatient procedure, so I was back home the same day. When it was time to leave the hospital, Jasmine circled around to pick me up at the entrance, where a nurse named Joe wheeled me out to the curb in a wheelchair. "Hey, Sis. Get in. You look weird with that eye patch." Jasmine always was a tease with me. It cheered me up to have her jousting me.

"Sure, I'll get in. Just give me a minute," I retorted. The nurse smiled as he assisted me into Jasmine's Toyota Corolla.

"Nice car," he commented, partially lifting me to set me into the passenger seat.

"Thanks. I like it too," Jasmine replied. We settled in for the ride from Portland to Corvallis. I was still groggy from the anesthesia, so conversation was limited. We arrived in about an hour and a half, with Jasmine taking my elbow as I got out of the car. "Okay, Cass, let's get you settled in the apartment. I'll bet Dominican will be glad to see you."

"Yeah, yeah. I'm okay," I insisted, as she still held onto my arm, and we made our way slowly into the apartment. Dominican was waiting at the door and brushed up against my leg, purring in anticipation. Jasmine spent the next two nights with me, preparing meals, and fluffing my pillow. It was nice to have her around. I felt so appreciative of her attention and love. For all our past times of harsh words, she was, after all, a good and kind sister. She left after the weekend, with promises to call and check on me for the next week or so.

The doctor said that I wouldn't know the outcome as far as improved vision for about a month. I was a bit nervous about that part, but Luis called daily, reassuring me that it would be okay. He also kept urging me to go to counseling, so I scheduled counseling for the PTSD I was still experiencing. It felt good to finally take positive steps in self-care also. Before I knew it, the one-month post op appointment arrived, and with it, I was beginning to see shapes and color in my operated eye.

Doctor Schmidt examined my eye thoroughly, and then pushed back her chair. She looked at me steadily and commented, "I think you will get back at least sixty percent vision. I will prescribe glasses after you visit again in another month to help with another twenty percent." She smiled encouragingly. "I consider the surgery a success, whereas you had no vision before, and now you should have the sixty percent."

"Okay, Dr. Schmidt. So, how long before I get the sixty percent? What is it now?"

"I would say it's at about forty percent now. I should think in another month you will get the full benefit of the surgery."

"Thank you, doctor." I left, not knowing whether to feel elated or disappointed. At least, I had sight now. That was a plus.

Eventually, I realized I had to face the prospect of setting a wedding date. As I became stronger both emotionally, from continued counseling, and physically, as I healed from the surgery, the idea seemed more plausible. I would be ready to plan soon. It was already late October when my eye fully healed, and I received new eyeglasses.

LUIS CONTINUED TO CALL EACH DAY, ENCOURAGING ME. I allowed myself to be genuinely happy for perhaps the first time in my life. We began making plans and set the wedding date in June of the following year, in 2012, which gave us both some needed time. We decided on a church wedding in Puebla, in the small chapel near his family's home. Luis' mother was elated at the idea of the wedding location, and even called me occasionally. She offered to help with the plans, and we would email one another picture ideas for flowers, wedding party attire, including my wedding dress, and food. In the meantime, Luis took a temporary position at a hospital in Puebla. As the wedding drew nearer, we hoped to decide where we would live as a couple. I was hoping for Oregon if he could make arrangements to pass medical certification requirements here.

There was still no one to give me away at the ceremony. I thought about my real father, and the old resentment flared up. It was disappointing to realize that he refused to share in my life. "You know, Cassie, it will all be okay. I'm sure that my father will stand in for you to escort you down the aisle."

"Luis, it won't be the same. I wish my father could be there. It's heartbreaking for me. Why can't he recognize me as his daughter?" I sniffed into the phone as we talked. I grabbed a tissue and dabbed my eyes. "It won't be the same—but I suppose it will have to do."

"It will still be nice, Cassie. Don't worry. I'll talk to my dad right away."

I wasn't sure how many of my own family would be able to make the trip to Mexico; Tully and Jasmine were planning to come, but no one else. As usual, I was the odd daughter of the family and would become married without the traditional crowd of family and friends. I tried not to let that dampen my mood in the preplanning of the wedding. I assured myself that I would soon have a new family—Luis' and his family.

Sun

Shoots of crocus and daffodil dare to peek
out from the soil,

The earth, soft underfoot from spring rains.

Squirrels titter from branches, relaying locations
of food to one another.

Robins busily gather soft dry grasses and twigs
for nests, future family homes.

Farmers till the ground, confident of the growth
of crops from the warming sun's rays.

Children burst outdoors, shouting their joy
at the clear skies,

While adults walk briskly, admiring the start
of spring, the promise of summer days.

Chapter 41

2012

Luis called every day and before long, spring arrived. The wedding day drew nearer, and with it, my anxiety increased. I poured myself into my work, which helped me to forget about wedding plans. I heard from Claire as well as Preston and Tommy, who were all planning to attend our wedding in Mexico. At least, I would have a few friends there besides my family, consisting of only Tully and Jasmine. The guy at work, Jason, caught on that I was engaged and finally left me alone. Since I was taking a leave from work, and didn't know for sure when I would return, the paper ran a short piece on my upcoming nuptials, including date and place of the chapel in Puebla. In May, the paper hired a temporary journalist to replace me during my leave. I began training her, and at that point, reality set in: I was really getting married.

I tossed and turned at night—my mind relentlessly going over details of the wedding. The PTSD continued, even though I still attended counseling sessions. Panic overtook me in a rush at odd moments. I worked overtime, trying to fill my brain with local news stories. The temporary journalist, Alicia, required my time as well, and I supervised and proofed her articles before she submitted them. As my sleep continued to dwindle, I felt more and more fatigued.

On a Tuesday morning, I awoke from a fitful dream. My head was hot and spinning, my body ached, and I couldn't swallow. I stumbled into the bathroom as nausea overtook me. I narrowly made it to the toilet, but I didn't vomit. Then I examined my arms. They were red from a rash which spread to my chest and legs. I called in sick, and worried about what to do. As I flopped back onto the bed once more, barely able to take care of myself, Dominican jumped up to check on me. He curled up next to me and purred loudly. "Thanks, Dominican. Your support helps a lot. What do I do now?" I rested awhile, petting Dominican's head while he droned on, and then managed to stumble into the kitchen to make some tea. I nibbled on a piece of dry toast and contemplated. Soon, I dialed my doctor's office, and enumerated my symptoms to the receptionist. She scheduled me to come in later that afternoon.

As it turned out, three days after the doctor ran tests, a nurse called to report that I had mononucleosis. While waiting for test results, I stayed home, trying to get stronger—which didn't seem to be working. Luis called on the second day of my illness. "Why didn't you let me know you were sick? What the heck? Aren't we engaged? I need to be told these things," he complained good naturedly.

There was no treatment, the nurse said, except for rest and a good diet. I didn't have the time for rest, and a good diet was not my strong point. Dutifully, I called Luis after the nurse let me know. "So, now we know. You need a good diet and lots of rest."

"I know, Luis. I got the lecture from the nurse. What can I do? I have to train my replacement, write my own stories, and prepare for our wedding." I took a deep breath, feeling overwhelmed and tired just at the thought of trying to do all of that. I lay down on the sofa while holding my phone, and Dominican nestled in beside me.

"So, get your replacement up and going now instead of waiting for when you leave for the ceremony. As far as wedding plans, just let Mom take over. She will be absolutely thrilled." Luis chuckled, picturing his mother's elation at being allowed to run freely with her nuptial ideas. "As for you, stay home and rest. Period."

Chapter 42

"Mom, what do you think? Why am I having these panic attacks? Do I call off the wedding or go through with it?" I sniffed and grabbed a tissue with my left hand, my right cradling the phone. I sat on the sofa with Dominican on my lap, his deafening rumble comforting me.

"Well," Tully replied, hesitating. "So, what made you agree to marry Luis in the first place? Think back to that moment. Where were you, and what were you doing at that time?"

"I would have to say that I agreed to sort of consider marrying him, and then was sure of it after we attended a mass service in Puebla. We went out to eat afterward and talked about it. Yes, I felt definitely sure then. There was a peace—a serenity while we prayed there in the cathedral. I felt happy, actually, for the first time in my life." I surprised myself with this answer.

"Okay then. You felt happiness, peace, and were sure of it, am I right?"

"Well, yeah, I did. But now? What do I do with these doubts now?"

"Cassie, Cassie. You always were the one to try to analyze everything. Do you love Luis?"

"Yes—of course I do."

"And how do you picture your future? Alone, with Luis, or with someone else?" I drew in a breath, thinking how to answer. Moments passed, and neither of us spoke. "Cassie? What are you thinking?"

"Well, about Luis. He's wonderful, Mom. I love him." I suddenly realized that I wasn't crying anymore. My sniffling stopped.

I grabbed a glass and filled it with water, cradling the phone with my left shoulder.

"So, how do you feel about that? Ready to tie the knot then? I don't want to give you the answer. You have to search your heart."

"My heart just gets muddled and confused with so many things going on. I still feel weak and sick, too. But thanks, Mom. I may have the answer now. I'll be alright."

"Good. Call me anytime. Love you, Cassie."

"Love you too, Mom." I hung up, petted Dominican, and got up to put on some water for tea. Then I dialed Luis.

The wedding plans continued, with Maria, Luis' mother, in charge, for the most part. I grew stronger gradually; it wasn't an easy recovery. When I returned for a follow up doctor visit, the doctor said that getting over mono took time for many people who were run down to begin with. I just hoped I would be physically up to the travel when the wedding date drew near.

Chapter 43

As the plane set down, its wheels touching Mexican soil, I felt restless. Here I was, arriving in Mexico City, to travel on to Puebla, the scene of my wedding. My wedding. The reality made me jittery, and I twisted up the napkin from my complimentary cookie. *You're going to be fine. It will be okay.* I told myself over and over, standing up to retrieve my carryon from the overhead bin. I pictured the lacey ivory gown stowed away in my checked bag. I smiled to myself, remembering how I looked in the mirror at the store where I purchased it in Portland. It was perfect for me, emphasizing my bare, cinnamon shoulders, the bodice well above any cleavage. The effect was both dramatic and demure. Nervous and excited, I deplaned, winding through the terminal to customs. Luis awaited me outside by the bus departures. When I arrived at that location, there he was, his eyes lighting up as he saw me approach. He strode swiftly to me, grabbed my luggage, and embraced me in one swift movement.

"Welcome back, Cassie. I've missed you so." Luis kissed me soundly on the lips, turning toward the bus we were to catch to Puebla. "My family is so excited, Cassie. Wait until you see them!" He turned his head to grin at me, but I still felt breathless, saying nothing. "Cassie, are you alright? You haven't spoken to me yet."

"Yes, yes! I am glad to see you and to finally be here. It—it was a bumpy flight," I excused myself lamely. Truth be told, I was happy to see him. I was just a bit overwhelmed that this was it—I would soon be wed here, in a foreign country. Luis took my hand and helped me board the bus after handing over the luggage to the driver. We hopped on board and took our seats near the front. A server walked along offering the customary juice and cookies. I didn't feel like eating but took the proffered mango juice and crisp cookies. Luis did as well. At least it would help pass the time as we traveled. Soon the bus lumbered out and onto the highway; gradually, the landscape changed from bustling city to countryside. I said as little as possible, nodding as Luis chattered excitedly about Maria's preparations for the big day, which was just a week away.

THE TAXI PULLED UP IN FRONT OF LUIS' PARENTS' HOME. We jumped out and the driver handed us my suitcases. The door to the house flew open at that moment, and Maria dashed out, followed by Mercedes and Viviana. Arms held wide, they all embraced me at once. I was smothered by kisses on both cheeks. "Welcome home, Cassie," Maria said, tears of happiness streaming down her face. "We have looked forward to your arrival. Come in." I was practically carried in by the hugging females, while Luis trailed behind with all my bags. As I stepped inside the house Maria asked, "When can we expect your mother and sister to arrive? And your friends?"

"Well, uh, my family will be here in three days. My friends will get here just the day before the wedding."

"Good, good. And do they need a place to stay? They are welcome here." Maria smiled, and Mercedes and Viviana nodded too.

"Thank you. They have reservations at the El Royalty Hotel downtown. No worry. Thank you so much." I checked my phone and noticed that Claire and Preston had sent messages confirming their plans to be here in just five days, a bit sooner than originally planned. My nerves jangled when I read the news. It was fast becoming a reality—I would be Mrs. Mendez in barely a week!

At dinner in the Mendez home, my soon to be father-in-law, Esteban, smiled warmly over his coffee. "Cassie, I will be happy to escort you down the aisle to give you away to my son."

"Uh, thank you, Mr. Mendez," I answered, feeling a bit odd at the irony of him "giving" me away to Luis. I realized it was just a formality, but still, it seemed weird. "It's nice of you to offer to do that, since my adoptive father is no longer living."

"Yes, well, I'm sorry for your loss. We all welcome you to our family. What better way to do that, right?" Esteban's expression was truly warm and inviting. They all seemed so glad I would be a part of their family soon. Maria and the sisters tittered excitedly as they brought in the sorbet for dessert.

"We can hardly wait. It will be beautiful for sure," Maria nodded as she spoke. We had all decided to go with emerald green as the main color, with pink and white bouquets of carnations, peonies, and roses. The verdant hue would accent Jasmine's complexion and strawberry blonde hair, as she would be my matron of honor. The sisters, Mercedes and Viviana, would also wear the green hue as bridesmaids. I had secretly hoped that Claire would be part of the wedding; however, I realized it was to be a family affair. With my illness, I didn't do very much of the actual planning. Luis asked his good friend and a couple of others from the university to be best man and groomsmen. They would continue the emerald theme with their ties and pocket kerchiefs. It all sounded grand and nice—too nice for my simple taste, but Maria had it all under control. No wonder I had the nervous twitches and uneasy stomach. This was almost too much for me. Hopefully, I would come through in one piece.

I was still sad that my biological dad would have nothing to do with me. In my imagination, my father would escort me down the aisle, turning to me and smiling proudly. I further envisioned my father, happy and handsome, as an older man, outfitted in his tux. My dark skin matched his, as we were father and daughter for sure. The dream evaporated and reality took over. It was nice that Luis' dad offered to do the honors of escorting me., but it just wasn't the same as if my father were here. I fervently wished that my good friend, Claire could have been in the wedding party, but Maria was so thrilled to have Luis' sisters in it, that I didn't say anything. At least, Jasmine would be there for me.

As the days ticked off, soon Tully and Jasmine arrived. Luis and I met them at the hotel. Both made a rush for me in the lobby and enveloped me in their hugs. "Cassie, I'm so happy to be here for this! I can't believe you are really getting married!" Mom gazed at me in wonder.

"Me too!" Jasmine chimed in. "You look great!"

"Th-thanks," I stammered. "I'm really nervous, though."

"Oh, what bride isn't. It's a big step, and lots of preparations for the day make it loom large." Tully stepped back to see me better. "You'll be okay."

"Right, you will," Jasmine assured me, her own wedding already in the rear mirror of her life. Luis had said nothing yet, just hung in the corner of the lobby, grinning at us all.

"Come over here, you handsome man," Tully said, grabbing his arm and pulling him close. Jasmine took his other arm, affectionately pulling him into our circle. Luis hugged them in return, pleased at their affections.

We decided to dine together in the hotel dining room, and chatted for over an hour, going over our plans for the big day. Just having Mom and Jasmine there helped me to unwind and feel a bit surer of myself. They were here for me, and soon, Claire, Preston, and Tommy would be as well.

THE NEXT DAY, WHEN CLAIRE AND PRESTON ARRIVED, I was surprised to see that now they were not only friends, but a couple. Luis and I, along with Tully and Jasmine, met them in the hotel lobby just minutes after they had checked in and gotten room keys. As they walked in, arm in arm, they turned to look into one another's eyes. Preston gave Claire a quick kiss on the lips. Tommy trailed along behind them, grinning sheepishly.

"What the heck? When did this happen?" I laughed merrily, now realizing why they had chosen to take the same flight to Mexico City.

"Oh, our constant phone calls regarding your adventures got to us. We decided to start dating and see where it went, didn't we?" Claire turned to Preston again, this time giving him the kiss. Tommy still hadn't said anything.

"I love it! Another couple like Luis and me with different cultures."

"Yep. Guess you could say that, although my family has lived in Frisco a long time, you know," Preston returned. "Several generations, in fact."

"Well, great. I love having you three here; makes me feel less alone and nervous. Thanks for coming."

"We wouldn't miss it; you know that," Claire said, grabbing Preston's hand as we headed toward the hotel dining area.

"I agree," Tommy finally commented. "I'm glad we can be here for you."

Chapter 44

The taxi picked us up to head to the wedding chapel. Tully and Jasmine rode with me, since Jasmine, as matron of honor, helped me to dress and do my hair. I was as nervous as a mother cat, and I didn't know how I would handle the day. I was so thankful to have my mom and sister with me, as well as Claire, who would meet up with us at the church. Luis would arrive separately, along with the men in the wedding party. Preston and Tommy arranged to go with Luis as well. "Do I look okay, Jas?" I patted my hair and peered in a hand mirror to check my lipstick.

"You look gorgeous, doesn't she, Mom?"

"Oh, absolutely! I am so proud of you, dear," Mom said, patting my knee, which was buried under layers of ivory satin and lace.

"I don't know. I can hardly wait for the champagne to settle my nerves," I said, giggling.

"In due time, sweetie. We have to get you through the ceremony first." Tully smiled, looking regal in her emerald green dress with capped sleeves. She wore a small net hat, perched over her red hair, serving as a head covering for entering the church. The effect suited her. Jasmine looked glamorous in her bare-shouldered green dress, also with long sleeves like my bridal gown. We crammed into the cab with our dresses billowing around our laps. The taxi driver glanced at us to make sure we were tucked in, and slammed the doors shut. He drove like a maniac, as if we were going to be late for my own wedding. I had noticed from other taxi rides here in Puebla, all drivers raced to their destinations no matter the occasion. It was unnerving, to say the least. Tully noticed my anxiety. "Uh, driver, could you slow down a bit? Our bride here is stressing out.

"Sorry, mam', I always drive this way. I have another pick up after I let you out." He continued his breakneck speed, and before long, we arrived at the church safely.

Claire was already inside, pacing the floor at the entrance. "Oh good, you're here," she breathed, obviously relieved. "The priest is asking questions about where you want to stand to take your vows. I didn't know what to tell him."

"Oh, well, I don't know either. Can't he ask Luis?"

"I'll go look for him. You need to go to this room over here to the side, and not let Luis see you until he meets you at the altar."

"Right she is," Tully chimed in. "Bad luck for him to see you today until that moment." Jasmine nodded in agreement, the two of them pushing me toward the door to the room where I was to wait for the ceremony to begin. As I entered, I noticed that some of Luis' family and friends were already arriving and taking their seats. My hands felt clammy from nervousness, so I smoothed them over the skirt of my dress. Soon, Mercedes and Viviana, along with Maria, burst into the waiting room, all smiles, chattering away in Spanish.

"Oh, Cassie, you look BEA-U-TI-FUL!" Maria exclaimed, all three rushing to me at once, oohing and ahhing over my gown, patting my bare shoulders. The sisters hugged me at the same moment, crushing my veil. Jasmine stepped in to adjust it, smiling, but saying nothing. I saw a few tears in her eyes as she moved up close to my face, repositioning the veil.

"Yes, you look so lovely, Cassie," she whispered, barely loud enough for the rest to hear.

"Thanks, Jas. Your opinion is important to me. Do you really think the dress suits me?" I still felt the jitters; I wanted her reassurance above anyone else's, since she was always so critical of me as we grew up.

"Oh, Cassie, absolutely. You are gorgeous, elegant, and yet you. It's perfect!"

"Okay. So why do I feel so anxious, so out of place?"

"Well, all of us felt that on our wedding day. It's normal, right, Mom?"

"Why yes, of course, Cassie. Your sister is right about that. I remember wanting to run out of the church for a breath of fresh air, but my mother made me stay. It was okay after the ceremony began. It's just pre-ceremony jitters. Don't worry."

"All right. But I don't like it. I'm at least going to peek outside the door of this stuffy room." I sauntered over toward the door, my skirt swishing as I moved. I peeked, and saw Luis and his father, Esteban, talking to a tall, dark man in a black suit with his back to me. All three seemed very serious. I gasped; my uneasiness kicked up a notch. What is going on here? My inner antenna was alerted, and my breaths came in uneven jags.

"Cass, are you alright?" Jasmine touched my shoulder, drawing closer to my face. "You look like you just saw a ghost."

"I—I did. You won't believe it. Go out there and stand by Luis for me, will you, Jas? Then come right back and tell me who you see." I shut the door at that moment, my breath catching in my throat. Before Jasmine could reopen the door, there was a gentle knock. Panicked, I fled to the corner of the small room, a foreboding feeling coming over me. "Jas, will you get the door? I'll wait here."

"What on earth? What's wrong, Sis? Okay, no worry." Jasmine swung the door open, and Robert Harris towered in the doorway. Jasmine, of course, had no idea who he was. "Yes? May I help you? Are you one of Luis' guests?" Jasmine stared at him, not knowing what to do. "The bride is in here, and no one may see her until the ceremony begins. Guests are supposed to take a seat in the chapel area." Jasmine pointed in the direction of the sanctuary.

"Uh, actually, miss, I'm here to see the bride to be, Casandra." Robert's sonorous, baritone voice shattered the silence in the room. "It's urgent." I shrank as far as I could in the furthermost corner. What in the world? Why is he here? He rejected me out of hand at the mountain top after I searched so hard to find him. Has he come all this way to ridicule me or forbid me to marry? I just want to get married in peace—if I can bring myself to get over my qualms.

Chapter 45

> "Happiness is like a butterfly: the more you chase it,
> the more it will elude you, but if you turn your attention to
> other things, it will come and sit softly on your shoulder."
>
> —Henry David Thoreau

Time stood still as my eyes met those of Robert Harris. Jasmine floated to my side, a questioning expression searching my face. "Why are you here?" I asked, my voice breaking.

Mom also joined me in the corner of the room, protectively guarding me. "Who is this?" Tully asked aloud.

Before I could answer, he spoke again. "Sorry for the intrusion. I am Casandra's father, Robert Harris. I read about the upcoming nuptials online in the newspaper Casandra works for." He advanced into the room, loping towards me. "Casandra, may I speak to you?" He must have noticed the fear in my eyes, adding, "Don't worry. Uh, I'll just ask you in front of everyone since you seem anxious."

"Yes, please, Mr. Harris. I am Tully McMillen, Cassie's adoptive mother. You can speak in front of me and Jasmine, her sister," she said, her head nodding towards Jasmine. Luis' mother and sisters took the cue and started walking towards the door to leave the room.

"It's okay. You may stay here as well, I'm sure," he assured them, turning to smile at the three ladies. They all looked over to me, awaiting my instruction.

"Uh, yes, please stay. What he has to say can be said in front of us all." I stood, twisting the fabric of my dress between my fingers, nervously waiting.

Robert Harris stepped closer to me, the ladies moving backward to give him space. "Casandra, I'm so sorry. When you showed up out of nowhere on the mountain top, it was such an unlikely place where no one would ever think to look. I didn't know what to think. Then, when I watched from my cabin window, I saw you mount your horse and ride away. I knew you were riding away from my life forever." He paused, taking me in from head to toe before continuing. "At that moment, I experienced an overwhelming realization of how much I had missed and how much I loved you. I had tried to forget but seeing you there face to face unlocked the memory of fathering a child. It was an unfamiliar emotion to have that feeling toward you. All those years… you were an unknown concept—an abstract idea. I had never seen you, even as a newborn. I had no idea that you would look anything like me. There you were, on my mountaintop hideaway—my own beautiful daughter." As he uttered the word 'daughter', his voice broke. I was unmoving, a statue, except as I silently twisted my gown. I noticed the tears that formed in the corners of his eyes. Still, I remained motionless.

My father's eyes. As I formed the word "father" in my brain, droplets fell onto my cheeks. He reached for the handkerchief in his suit pocket and dabbed at his eyes. Then he held out the handkerchief to me, his daughter. With my father's tears soaked into the kerchief, I took it, and wiped my cheeks. Our tears mingled, those of my father and mine. My hand felt the moistness of the fabric, and more tears gushed out. As I used the handkerchief once more, I heard the soft sniffling of all the women in the room. Someone must have grabbed a tissue box, because soon, everyone had a tissue, and was wiping at her face. Robert Harris moved closer; his head bowed. I still had not moved, the emotions of anger, regret, happiness, uncertainty, and the questioning of why, all coursing through my mind. But the weeping overcame it all.

"Casandra, I came to ask you something. I know that I wasn't there for you all those years—your whole life, in fact." At that, he paused, the tears dropping freely onto his tie. He drew a ragged breath and continued. "But I'm here for you now. If you'll have me, and if you'll forgive me. Will you?" His eyes met mine, and both of us continued to weep softly. "I would be honored if you would allow me to walk you down the aisle to give you away. But I want you back, as well. I want you for the rest of my life, to be the father that you so deserved to have." He stood, hands outstretched as if in surrender, crying openly. I was shocked; dumbfounded. How do I respond? I just looked at him again, crying softly, my hands at my sides, fingers furiously twisting my dress.

"Casandra," he continued, " You are my butterfly. When you left that day, I realized that you are the butterfly for which I was searching for my entire life. I knew from that moment on the mountaintop that you are so much like me, searching constantly for the elusive—the butterfly. Before that moment, I never understood myself—why I had to keep searching, to continue researching. Now I know. You and I, we have to understand ourselves." He smiled and stepped a tiny bit closer. "Is it too late to show you that?" He took the kerchief from me, blotting at his face. "I'll never abandon you again if you'll have me. If you'll allow me this privilege to take your arm down the aisle."

I still didn't move. I was speechless, and I knew the tears had smudged my makeup on this, my wedding day. Why was I obsessing over makeup? My mind flashed back to a lifetime of hurt, of rejection from birth by both biological parents, but I was moved to tears anyway.

"Before you answer, I want to assure you that I have both your future husband's and father-in-law's permission to escort you today. Take your time with the rest, with allowing me to become a part of your future. Just please allow me this today." He looked so vulnerable—pathetic and lonely.

I took a step towards him, reaching the nearness of his chest, and he extended his arms to embrace me. "Y—yes. Of course. You traveled a long way for this. Yes, please…. Dad." I wrapped my arms around him, my face buried in his shoulder. He smelled of a woodsy, exhilarating aftershave. My father's cologne. Totally pleasant—like coming home. "Thank you for coming, Dad," I whispered, closing my eyes, and sensing a feeling I had never experienced before: the comforting arms of my biological father. I had searched for so long and yearned for this ever since I had been born. We had a long way to go, but at least, this was the first step. Hopefully, the first of many happy times. "And yes, I forgive you. I—I love you, too," I added softly, my voice cracking.

I'm not sure how long we held the embrace, but at long last, Jasmine tapped my shoulder. "Uh, sorry to interrupt, but perhaps I could help you touch up your makeup, Sis." Jasmine looked like she could use a touch up as well, as she continued to press her eyes with a tissue. Awkwardly, my father and I broke off the hug.

"So, this must be your beautiful sister," he said, turning to greet her with a smile and handshake.

"Yes, my name is Jasmine. So glad you are here for Cassie." At that, she gave a side hug to Robert Harris, my real father. My missing father for all these years, here for my wedding day. I truly felt like I had come home. A butterfly who had fluttered around the U.S. and Mexico and had at long last, arrived home. Home with my father, my dad.

EPILOGUE

June 2017

> "Just when the caterpillar thought the world was over it became a butterfly."
>
> —LEWIS CARROLL, ALICE IN WONDERLAND

The wedding went off smoothly after Dad and I had our heartfelt conversation in the dressing room. Luis and I reflected on that as we sat on deck chairs and watched the waves roll in. We had moved to Dr. Jordan's beach house two years after we married. Luis had passed the medical certifications to practice in the U.S. after also receiving his American citizenship. He took over the practice of a retiring doctor here at Lincoln City. I, of course, eventually landed a reporter position with the local paper. Shortly after our wedding, Preston and Clair announced their engagement, and were married within six months. I was her matron of honor, and Tommy, the best man.

Today was our fifth wedding anniversary. Luis took my hand as we sat, glasses of Perrier resting on a small table in front of us. "So, Cassie, when did you say your father is arriving?"

"Well, his plane is due to arrive in Portland tomorrow at 2:00. We should leave here in the morning around 11:00 to be there in time." I reached down to my feet where old Dominican was curled into a ball. He looked up, purring contentedly. "Dominican, you will get to meet my father. My real father. Think of that." I grinned, Dominican continuing to purr, using my foot as a pillow. "So, what do you think, Luis? Will Dominican accept the new baby when she arrives?" I looked to Luis, and he reached over to pet the cat as well.

"Sure. He's a people lover. He'll probably become the next nanny cat; don't you think?" I had forgotten that I told Luis about my childhood cat, Penelope, who served as the nanny cat to my sister and me.

I chuckled, pleased that Luis remembered I had told him that once. "Right! You're right, of course! Dominican will love her. I can hardly wait to tell Dad the news. He'll have to return again when the baby is born. Just before Thanksgiving time. He can stay here, and I'll cook." Luis raised an eyebrow and looked at me. He knew my culinary skills weren't the best. "Or not. We could go to Mom's perhaps. Tully loves to host Thanksgiving."

"Sure, sure. Let's see how it goes by then. In the meantime, I love you, my bride." He patted my knee affectionately. I sat content, listening to the waves washing to shore, relaxing my mind and spirit, the quest to find my father forever completed. I was truly home after searching all those years. I realized now that I was fortunate to have my adoptive mother and sister and her two children, my niece and nephew. Now I had my husband, Luis, and his family, Dr. Jordan's beach house, and Dominican. Best of all, I had at long last found my real father, who would arrive here soon. Home at last.

Acknowledgements

I would like to thank the nature guides who work or volunteer for the South Padre Island Birding and Nature Center in South Padre Island, Texas. Their expertise and information regarding the island's wildlife; in particular, birds and butterflies, native plants, and eco system, were an invaluable resource for this book. The birding center offers daily tours and informational lectures which are open to the public.

Anyone interested may go to the website at: www.spigirding.com.

Thank you to Raul Villalva for his helpful ideas and firsthand knowledge of the areas of Mexico mentioned in this novel.

A special thank you goes to Marlene Loisdotter for her invaluable expertise, encouragement, and editing advice. Her ongoing inspiration is a motivating force in our writing group.

Appreciation is extended to everyone in our weekly writing group for their pithy comments and helpful ideas as I worked on this writing endeavor. A big thank you is also sent to friends and family for their positive support and faith in me as a writer. For all of you, I am grateful.

Bibliography

Butterfly quotes from: www.butterflywebsite.com/butterfly-quote.cfm

www.Mexperience.com/travel/outdoors/monarch-butterflies-mexico/

www.monarchhighway.org

www.monarchjointventure.org

www.monarch.org

public domain map: https://pichryl.com/media/north-america-3 available through Library of Congress

www.sciencealert.com/theworld-s-largest-pyramid-is-hidden-under-a-mountain-in-mexico

www.spibirding.com

www.theorginaldolphinwatch.com

Wikipedia: Great Pyramid of Cholula

Author's Note

Personal Travel as Resource

My personal travels have taken me to many places, but for the intentions of this novel, some were helpful as resources for the story. I have toured numerous locations in Mexico, and among those mentioned in the narrative, the cities of Puebla and Cholula. I found the countless churches and enormous cathedrals staggering, and have attempted, in this story, to portray them as the historical icons that they are. I ascended to the summit of the pyramid in Cholula, encountering the view in the distance of the mountain peaks of Popocatepetl and Iztaccihuatl.

In the city of Puebla, a former Spanish colony, I toured the downtown area and observed colonial historic buildings such as the city hall area and stunning cathedral.

I journeyed to South Padre Island, Texas in 2019, primarily to witness the butterfly migration in October, and to participate in the annual Monarch Butterfly Festival held at the South Padre Island Birding and Nature Center. I toured a rescue center and hospital for injured sea turtles, as well as took a sunset boat cruise to observe the dolphins. All of these experiences supplemented the creation of this novel.

www.ingramcontent.com/pod-product-compliance
Lightning Source LLC
LaVergne TN
LVHW041628060526
838200LV00040B/1481